J.T. EDSON'S FLOATING OUTFIT

The toughest bunch of Rebels that ever lost a war, they fought for the South, and then for Texas, as the legendary Floating Outfit of "Ole Devil" Hardin's O.D. Connected Ranch.

MARK COUNTER was the best-dressed man in the West: always dressed fit-to-kill. BELLE BOYD was as deadly as she was beautiful, with a "Manhattan" model Colt tucked under her long skirts. THE YSABEL KID was Comanche fast and Texas tough. And the most famous of them all was DUSTY FOG, the ex-cavalryman known as the Rio Hondo Gun Wizard.

J. T. Edson has captured all the excitement and adventure of the raw frontier in this magnificent Western series. Turn the page for a complete list of Berkley Floating Outfit titles.

J. T. EDSON'S FLOATING OUTFIT WESTERN ADVENTURES FROM BERKLEY

THE YSABEL KID
SET TEXAS BACK ON HER FEET
THE HIDE AND TALLOW MEN
TROUBLED RANGE
SIDEWINDER
McGRAW'S INHERITANCE
THE BAD BUNCH
TO ARMS, TO ARMS, IN DIXIE!
HELL IN THE PALO DURO
GO BACK TO HELL
THE SOUTH WILL RISE AGAIN
.44 CALIBER MAN
A HORSE CALLED MOGOLLON
GOODNIGHT'S DREAM
FROM HIDE AND HORN
THE HOODED RIDERS
QUIET TOWN
TRAIL BOSS
WAGONS TO BACKSIGHT
RANGELAND HERCULES
THE HALF BREED
THE WILDCATS
THE FAST GUNS
CUCHILO
A TOWN CALLED YELLOWDOG
THE TROUBLE BUSTERS
THE LAW OF THE GUN
THE PEACEMAKERS
THE RUSHERS
THE QUEST FOR BOWIE'S BLADE
THE FORTUNE HUNTERS
THE TEXAN
THE RIO HONDO KID
RIO GUNS
GUN WIZARD
TRIGGER FAST
RETURN TO BACKSIGHT
THE MAKING OF A LAWMAN
TERROR VALLEY
APACHE RAMPAGE
THE RIO HONDO WAR
THE FLOATING OUTFIT
THE MAN FROM TEXAS
GUNSMOKE THUNDER
THE SMALL TEXAN
THE TOWN TAMERS
GUNS IN THE NIGHT
WHITE INDIANS
WACO'S DEBT
OLD MOCCASINS ON THE TRAIL
THE HARD RIDERS
THE GENTLE GIANT
THE TRIGGER MASTER
THE TEXAS ASSASSIN
THE COLT AND THE SABRE
THE DEVIL GUN

J.T. Edson

THE DEVIL GUN

BERKLEY BOOKS, NEW YORK

This Berkley book contains the complete
text of the original edition.
It has been completely reset in a typeface
designed for easy reading and was printed
from new film.

THE DEVIL GUN

A Berkley Book/published by arrangement with
Transworld Publishers Ltd.

PRINTING HISTORY
Corgi edition published 1968
Berkley edition/January 1987

For information address: Transworld Publishers Ltd.,
Century House, 61–63 Uxbridge Road,
Ealing, London W5 5SA, England.

ISBN: 0-425-09478-2

A BERKLEY BOOK® TM 757,375
Berkley Books are published by The Berkley Publishing Group,
200 Madison Avenue, New York, NY 10016.

PRINTED IN THE UNITED STATES OF AMERICA

CHAPTER ONE

Deserter—And Traitor

Ten months ago 2nd Lieutenant Jackson H. Marsden had been honour cadet of his year at West Point Military Academy. Only three months back he received a commendation for his handling of the rearguard action when the Federal forces met with a bloody repulse at Poison Springs. It had been but two weeks since his company commander gave Marsden a strong hint that he was marked for early and rapid promotion. Now he was a deserter and in the next few days, a week at most, would also be a traitor.

Yet it must be done. Loyalty to his country, or rather to the division of his country that he chose to serve, could not stand against the horrible results of the plan he chanced to discover. No man who lived out West—even a man in his early twenties—could fail to be deeply disturbed when contemplating the full meaning of that plan. The fools who spawned the scheme could have no idea of its full and true implications. Or they were so blinded by their bigotry and hatred of the Confederacy that they did not care what terrible and hideous situation their scheme bore in its wake. Marsden did not know which, ignorance or bigotry, accounted for the actions of the men behind the scheme, nor did he greatly care. All he knew was that he must do something to prevent the scheme's completion.

Born into a family of career soldiers, the decision to desert and become a traitor did not come easily. Already he had lost two brothers and several cousins in the bitter fighting of the Civil War. From his earliest days he had been trained in discipline and loyalty, taught that he must do his duty. He served well, putting aside his disappointment at being assigned to the 8th 'Stedloe's East Coast' Zouaves, an infantry regiment, when he hoped for a place in a cavalry unit, and gained distinction if only in the little-publicised campaign to bring Arkansas back into the Union.

At last he came face to face with a situation not envisaged in any military text book; something militarily and morally wrong—as far wrong as it was possible for inexperienced human beings to get—and he knew he must do something to correct the wrong.

Merely seeing his commanding officer and laying the facts before him would not do. Serving as one of the few regular officers in a volunteer regiment, Marsden knew how slight was the bond between himself and the volunteer officers. While Colonel Stedloe might be a brilliant businessman and showed some courage in action, he could hardly be expected to see all the ramifications of the scheme to which he gave his consent. A regular officer with experience in the West would have discarded the scheme when Captain Castle and Lieutenant Silverman presented it. Stedloe not only accepted the scheme, but gave it his full support and blessing. If he saw any lack of enthusiasm from his regular officers, he probably attributed it to jealousy, for little love was lost between the career soldiers and the amateurs who joined only to fight the South. Perhaps Marsden could have killed the scheme, but he was out of camp on outpost duty during its conception and the other three lacked experience on the frontier, so could not offer objections. In fact, seen with inexperienced eyes, the scheme had much to commend it and its successful conclusion could do much to not only hasten the end of the War, but also might easily bring about Union victory. The commanding general, no career soldier, would view it in that light.

Marsden, lacking support from his own kind, spent a sleepless night. By dawn he reached a decision. Saying nothing to anybody, not even to Rory McDougal, West Point companion and fellow career lieutenant in the Zouaves, he took his horse from the lines, used the ferry across the Arkansas River and rode west towards the Ouachita Mountains. That had been the previous morning and by now his absence must have been noticed. Of course Rory would cover up for him as long as possible, thinking he had gone to visit a charming young 'lady' of their acquaintance. Rory would never suspect Marsden of going over the hill, deserting, and might lay his disappearance to action by a fast-riding troop of Southern cavalry making a strike to beard the Union army in its Little Rock den. Maybe some of the volunteer officers would be suspicious, suspicion came naturally to their kind. Even now a search might be organised with the intention of bringing him back.

The thought brought misery to Marsden. No matter how this affair came out, his career in the Army was finished. A court martial, dismissal from the service at least, more likely a firing squad, awaited him—even if the Confederate Army believed his story and did not hold him as a prisoner-of-war.

With the Ouachita River ahead, apprehension by Union forces grew less while still remaining a possibility. Although the victory at Prairie Grove in December 1862, the capture of Arkansas Post, battle at Helena and fall of Little Rock in '63 put the Union in possession of all North-Eastern Arkansas, they made little progress in gathering the rest of the state from Confederate hands. In fact the

Union's defeats that year at Poison Springs, Mark's Mill, Pine Bluffs and Jenkins' Ferry had prevented further conquest of Arkansas. So the land between the Arkansas and Ouachita Rivers belonged to neither side and was the scene of many bloody skirmishes. The nearer one came to the Ouachita, the less chance of meeting Union forces; yet this also added to the chance of detection should one meet a Union patrol. So close to the Ouachita a lone officer would attract attention. While the Zouaves had given up their flashy uniforms—copied from the French-Algerian troops which gave them their name—and dressed as did most of the Union Army, it would take experienced men only a close glance to know that Marsden belonged to the infantry. No foot-soldier would be so close to the Ouachita River without written authority from his colonel, and certainly would not ride without an escort. If seen by a Union cavalry patrol, Marsden knew he could not think up a convincing story enough to prevent its commander taking him back for investigation and Colonel Stedloe was smart enough to guess at the reason for his lieutenant's presence on the river.

So Marsden rode slowly, keeping to low ground and avoiding sky-lines, alert all the time for hostile presences. Wending his way through the rolling, open country, he saw no sign of other human beings. However, he could not risk crossing at a ford or shallow stretch for such might be under Union surveillance. Knowing the Confederate cavalry's skill as raiders, the Union forces concentrated on preventing crossings of the Ouachita rather than attacking the rebels beyond the river, and kept watch on places where an easy crossing might be made.

Soon he came to the wooded country bordering the Ouachita and, with the sun beginning its downward slide to wards the western horizon, rode along the river bank searching for an available crossing place. At last he found a spot that might satisfy his needs. The tree-dotted banks dropped steeply on either side, the river forming a long, deep, slow-moving pool between them and offering no difficulty to a skilled man. Having seen no sign of life on either bank for the past hour, Marsden decided to make his crossing.

Before starting the descent, Marsden swung from his saddle, took out his field glasses and made a careful search of the surrounding country. He was a tall, slim young man, yet gave the impression of strength, with black hair and a ruggedly handsome face. As a result of his pretence of going to Little Rock when leaving camp Marsden wore his black Burnside felt hat, its right side turned up and fastened with his State's coat of arms insignia, the bugle badge of the infantry on its front, together with the regiment's number, and black plume curling up the right side. Instead of his comfortable field uniform, he wore a single-breasted dark blue frock coat with a stand-up collar; a sword belt carried his straight infantry sword and an Army Colt in a closed-top holster. Dark blue trousers with a one-eighth of an inch stripe of sky blue—the colour of the infantry—and well-shone Jefferson shoes completed the outfit. Not a dress a man would wear when riding on lawful patrol in the no-man's land between the Arkansas and Ouachita rivers.

All Marsden's early training had been concerned with cavalry work, so he knew how to handle a horse during swimming. First he stripped off his clothing and wrapped it carefully in his poncho. Strapping the protected bundle firmly to the saddle, he swung afork his bay horse and eased the animal down the slope. In a well-organised crossing, the horse would have been stripped of its saddle, the latter being ferried across along with the rider's property, but Marsden had to make do as best he could. He knew a horse was a powerful natural swimmer capable of carrying even a fully equipped man on its back for some considerable distance, so the bay would not be impeded or endangered by the saddle.

Not for the first time Marsden found himself blessing

his lessons in horsemanship as a boy, for they enabled him to select a fine mount and gave him the confidence and ability to handle the horse in any conditions. Before the horse took three steps down the slope, Marsden knew he would need all his ability. Not only did the slope prove to be deceptively steep, but the earth under the horse's hooves gave little support and began to shift beneath the animal. Feeling the horse's hooves churning and sliding, Marsden used all his skill to keep the bay under control and prevent it from a panic which might bring about a helpless slide down the slope at an ever-increasing speed.

Down went the man and horse, still a cohesive unit, with Marsden guiding his mount as well as he could, keeping it clear of the trees which grew on the slope. It said much for his skill on a horse that he kept the bay from crashing into any of the trees, although he grazed his bare legs on more than one occasion.

An instant too late Marsden made a shocking discovery. The slope fell away in a sheer drop of some twenty feet instead of coming down at an angle to join the river; something which could not be seen from the top of the bank. Man and horse saw the danger at the same moment. Throwing back his weight in the saddle, Marsden hauled back on the reins in a vain attempt to stop the downward slide. Then, seeing he could not halt the slide, he gave the horse its head. With the moving earth carrying it onwards, the horse gathered itself and launched out from the edge of the fall, as if trying to leap across the width of the Ouachita.

For a moment it seemed to Marsden that he and the horse hung suspended in the air, then the law of gravity took hold and they plunged down towards the river. Even as he gave a silent prayer that there might be enough water to break their fall, Marsden kicked his feet from the stirrup irons and thrust himself clear of the horse. Side by side they struck the water and Marsden felt himself going down, the icy chill biting into his naked body as the green-looking river swarmed over him. Deeper and deeper he went, until his feet hit the rocky bed of the river. He bent his knees, then thrust with his feet, propelling himself up towards the surface. Above him, he could see the bay's legs and body, with its reins trailing down. Marsden kicked out with his legs, driving himself forward and chancing a kick from the bay's churning hooves as he reached towards the reins. If the bay once got clear, he could not hope to catch up with it, strong swimmer though he was. The horse had been winded by the fall, but seemed to be recovering. Even as Marsden's hands closed on the slick leather of the reins, he felt the horse starting to swim. Then Marsden's head broke the surface. Desperately he clung to the reins and succeeded in slowing the horse sufficiently for him to swim close. A grab with his free hand caught hold of the bay's mane and he drew himself nearer to the horse.

Marsden found himself on the upstream flank of the horse, but realised that his mount had turned towards the shore they just left. While that was only to be expected, Marsden wanted to cross the river. When a horse swims, only its head remains in plain view, the rest of the body being just below the surface; so Marsden knew that the reins could not be used in steering the animal. He drew himself forward until the saddle partially supported his weight and while in that position managed to knot the reins in such a manner that they would not trail down and entangle the bay's legs. With that done, he slipped back into the water, clinging to the mane with his left hand. Scooping up a handful of water with his right, he splashed the bay's face. Twice he did this before the bay started to swing away from the east bank of the river. Not unnaturally the horse showed some reluctance to leave the land which lay so close to it, but Marsden continued splashing until he had his way and the bay's head pointed west. The current was negligible in the deep hole and so Marsden had no difficulty in keeping the horse pointed straight across the river. He found much the same formation of land at the other side, a sheer wall rising some twenty to thirty feet at the water's edge.

"We'll just have to take a chance, horse," he said gently and looked around.

As far as he could see, the wall continued for at least half a mile in either direction. The question arose of which way to go. After a moment's thought, Marsden allowed the horse to turn its head downstream. They might as well take advantage of what little current flowed through the deep pool, Marsden decided.

After the first shock of contact, the water was not too cold, but Marsden knew he must get out as soon as possible. With the sun setting, the temperature of the river would drop. Even now, the west bank being in shadow due to the setting sun, he could feel a chill creeping through him and knew it would become far worse as night set in.

Not for almost a quarter of a mile did any sign of relief come and even then it offered small comfort. A crack in the face of the wall led down to a shelf of dry rock which thrust out into the water. Eagerly the bay made for land and Marsden made no attempt to prevent it. Hooves sliding on the wet rock, the horse drew itself up onto solid ground and Marsden gratefully hauled himself out in the bay's wake.

Once ashore, the young officer looked around him and studied his position. The rocky out-crop on which he stood made a shelf some thirty feet long and fifteen wide, and the crack in the wall clearly went all the way to the top. This latter was proved by the animal dung which lay scattered about the rock, although no tracks could show upon such a hard surface. Marsden, a keen hunter, examined the different droppings with interest, recognising wapiti, Kansas whitetail deer and black bear faeces. Only the first and last of the trio interested Marsden at that moment, for a white tail could climb where no horse might follow. However, Marsden figured he ought to be able to take as sure-footed a horse as the bay anywhere either a bulky bull wapiti or a black bear managed to walk.

On further examination a chilling fact became plain to Marsden. The bear's droppings appeared to be much fresher than he cared to think about. While the black bear might not be as dangerous as a grizzly, meeting one in the confines of that crack would be mighty hectic for a man armed only with a sword and revolver.

Thinking of his weapons recalled to Marsden his state of undress and caused him to unstrap and open the poncho-wrapped bundle. Apparently the poncho's rubberised cloth fulfilled its manufacturer's advertising boasts, for none of the clothing gave any sign of dampness as he took them out. Using his undershirt as a towel, he dried himself swiftly and then dressed. With his weapon belt around his waist, the holster's top opened to allow easy access to the revolver butt, Marsden felt a little more contented. He checked on the bay's saddle, mounted and urged the horse up the steep slope of the crack.

Although the climb proved difficult, and called for skilled co-ordination between rider and mount, it did not bring out the added hazard of the black bear. Once out of the crack, the going proved much easier. Finding a slightly level piece of ground which offered grazing for his horse, Marsden dismounted. Already night had fallen and he decided to care for the horse before continuing with his search for a Confederate unit to which he could surrender.

With the bay grazing and its saddle-blanket hung out to dry, Marsden found himself with nothing to do but think; and with the thoughts came back misery. Crossing the Ouachita had been the end of any chance to withdraw from his plan. Up to then a fast ride would still have carried him back to safety and his absence could be put down to visiting Betty Mayhew in Little Rock. He knew he could rely on her to agree that he had been with her the whole time. At most Stedloe would have awarded his errant shavetail with a week of Officer of the Day duties. However, the time when Marsden could return had now passed. Nor, when he thought of the effects of Castle and Silverman's scheme, could Marsden turn back even if he knew for certain he would not be punished in any way for his absence.

The feeling of misery drove Marsden to forget his plan to stay in the small clearing until dawn. He checked the saddle blanket and found it to be dry enough for use. So he saddled the bay, mounted and rode off into the darkness. Holding his bay to a steady walk, he topped the west bank of the Ouachita and set off towards the rolling mountains.

Two hours went by without any sign of human beings. Marsden kept his horse at a steady walk and used his eyes. Just as he was thinking that it might be as well to halt for the night, he caught a glimpse of something red in the blackness to his right. Halting his horse, he turned his gaze in the direction but saw nothing. He wondered if his eyes might be playing tricks on him, but backing his horse a few steps brought the red glow into sight once more. A fire glowed among trees about half a mile or more away. From its appearance, Marsden concluded that its makers had no wish to be located. That in itself meant little. No troops on active service would willingly give away their position. However, it could mean danger. A raiding band of Union calvary were likely to take precaution with their fires and Marsden knew he must not ride blindly. Capture by the Union now meant certain and immediate death. No patrol raiding in enemy territory would burden itself with a deserter who clearly intended to search out and hand himself over to the enemy.

Only by winding about and keeping his eyes fixed on the partially hidden glow of the fire did Marsden manage to head in the required direction. At last he decided he could chance going no closer on his horse. Still he could not see what manner of people used the camp and so intended to make his scout on foot. Fortunately for him, the wind blew from behind him and towards the camp. There was no chance of his horse getting wind of any mounts the campers might have, and betraying Marsden's presence by whinneying a greeting to its kind.

After securing the bay to a tree, Marsden moved forward on foot. Anybody in that area of the Ouachita Mountains would most likely be a belligerent from one side or the other. Maybe Marsden would have sufficient luck to come into contact with a Confederate unit commanded by a man who would see the full import of his news and waste no time in directing him to the commanding general, or somebody who could make arrangements to halt Castle and Silverman's scheme.

Moving through darkened, wooded country in silence was no time for idle thought. Every instinct must be directed to the silent placing of feet and ensuring that nothing caught or rattled against the surrounding trees and bushes. Marsden threw off his thoughts and concentrated. From odd glimpses gained during his advance, Marsden decided that the camp must be set in a fair-sized clearing surrounded by thick bushes; an almost ideal location in that it offered good cover to the occupants and almost hid their fire from sight.

On silent feet Marsden eased closer to the camp, coming to a halt at the side of a large bush. Gently he parted a couple of branches and peered through the gap. At one side of the clearing stood a couple of lines of good horses, yet they had no guard watching them. A couple of bell tents, and a trio of hospital pattern tents were scattered about the clearing in a most unmilitary manner. Those two sights gave Marsden a warning that he must not fall into the hands of the people in the camp, even before he saw the occupants.

CHAPTER TWO

David O. Dodd's Sister

Crouching in his position behind the bush, Marsden turned his eyes to the occupants of the camp as they gathered about the fire. Not one of the party wore a uniform of any kind—unless he counted the occasional Union overcoat or tunic. In 1864, even with the U.S. Navy's blockade slowly strangling the South, the Confederate Army still kept its men in some semblance of uniform. The ten or so men around the fire wore head-dress ranging from coonskin caps to a good quality Burnside officer's hat, and sported civilian clothing as diverse as the head-wear. Only one thing had they in common, every man wore a pair of revolvers at his waist. None of them had shaved and all looked mean, cruel, vicious in the light of the flames. Marsden ignored the single woman at the fire, giving her hardly more than a single glance and discarding her as one of the usual type of camp follower to be found with such a band.

"Bushwhackers!" he mused. "I'd best get the hell out of here."

During the War many bands of irregulars fought on both

sides; if fought was the correct term for their activities. Unattached to any formal military organisation, the bushwhackers of the South and the Red-Legs of the Union looted and raided in the name of patriotism. Despised by the formal forces of the North and South, the various bands of irregulars ranged the strife-torn land, avoiding the real fighting. Even if Marsden knew which side claimed the party's so-called allegiance, he must not fall into their hands.

Even as the thought came to Marsden's head and he started to turn away, he heard the startled chatter of a disturbed bird. The soldier brought his head around towards the sound and saw a dark, human shape looming towards him. With no time to draw a weapon, Marsden shot out his fist, driving the gauntlet-covered knuckles full into his attacker's face. Although he changed the attacker's advance to a hurried retreat, Marsden knew he was not out of danger. He sensed rather than saw the second man coming in from the rear with arms widespread to grab him. Back shot Marsden's left arm, propelling the elbow savagely into the chest of the second attacker, bringing a gasping croak of pain and sending him stumbling away.

Surprised yells rose from the camp, but Marsden ignored the sounds. Just as he prepared to plunge away into the trees and make a dash for freedom, he saw yet a third bearded shape materialise close at hand. The fire's light glinted momentarily from the butt-plate of the carbine held by the third man as it swung up and drove down again. Too late Marsden tried to avoid the blow. His foot slipped and he felt the carbine's butt contact with the side of his hat. The force of the blow sent Marsden sprawling through the bushes and into the camp clearing where he landed on his knees. Snarling, gibbering almost in his rage, the first attacker crashed forward through the bushes after Marsden and launched a kick at the officer's head. Although Marsden tried to avoid the lashing boot, he only partially succeeded. He managed to move himself sufficiently far forward that his head missed the impact of the kick, but took it in his ribs instead. Pain knifed through Marsden and he pitched over, rolling on the ground.

Men sprang forward, catching Marsden by the arms and dragging him to his feet. Snarling curses through blood-dripping lips, the first attacker prepared to resume his assault.

"Let me at him!" screeched the man. "I want to see his blood."

"Now jest you hold it up there!" growled a commanding voice, and at its sound the man drew back.

Dazedly Marsden turned to look at the speaker. It figured, the big, burly man wearing the Burnside hat and good quality clothing was sure to be the leader of the Bushwhacker band. Swaggering forward, the man jerked a contemptuous thumb at Marsden and turned to the carbine-armed attacker who slouched forward on moccasin clad feet.

"Done saw him sneaking down on the camp," the man said without waiting for the obvious question. "Me'n the boys moved in on him. Done sent Milky to collect his hoss, Ashley."

A sick, sinking feeling hit Marsden as he heard the name. While not as famous, or notorious, as Bloody Bill Anderson, George Todd or William Clarke Quantrill—possibly due to their presence in a more publicised section of the fighting area—Wick Ashley's reputation was known to people in Arkansas. It was not a reputation to hearten a man unfortunate enough to fall into Ashley's hands.

"Drag him closer to the fire so's we can see what we got, boys," Ashley ordered.

"Wonder if there's more of 'em about?" asked the sentry, resting his Perry carbine on the crook of his arm.

"You'd best go see, Thad," suggested Ashley.

"Reckon I had at that," agreed the man and faded off into the bushes.

Walking back to where two of his men stood supporting

and restraining Marsden by the fire, Ashley looked the young soldier over as a farmer might study a prize bull.

"Fancy sword, cost good money," Ashley grunted and stepped forward to open Marsden's holster "New Army Colt too." He reached out to feel the material of the uniform, then examine the epaulets. "That's good broadcloth, and I'll swan if these doo-hickey ain't solid gold. Boots's hand-made too. Yes sir, boys, I reckon we caught us a good one there. I'll just bet his folks'll pay up without asking twice to get him back. Might even have enough cash-money back at his camp to have it done his-self and save time."

Among their other nefarious acts the irregulars ran a profitable side-line in offering such prisoners as they felt wealthy enough a chance to pay ransom for their freedom. Many of the bands had contacts on the enemy side who could notify the prisoner's friends or relations and arrange for the delivery of the ransom money. It seemed that Ashley possessed such a contact, for he showed complete confidence and did not need to think about disposing of his prisoner.

Cohesive thought returned to Marsden, forcing him to stand still instead of struggling against the restraining hands while his pockets were emptied. A snap of fingers and cold scowl caused one of the searchers to pass Marsden's well-filled wallet to Ashley. Looking into the wallet, Ashley ran an appreciative finger across the paper money it held. Marsden tried to struggle as a stocky, bearded tough hauled out his father's watch from under the tunic, but the men holding him tightened their grip and kept him immobile.

"Allus wanted a gold watch," grinned the man and turned to Ashley. "It's my turn to take first pick at his gear."

"Have I argued?" inquired Ashley and the man held the watch to an ear before stuffing it away into his pocket. Ashley swung his attention back to Marsden. "How's about it, soldier boy. You got anybody'd pay to get you back safe and well?"

"I—I've got to be taken to a Confederate unit," Marsden answered.

"We're a Confederate unit, boy," scoffed Ashley.

"I mean regulars."

"Now ain't we good enough to suit you?" sneered the bushwhacker leader.

"I tell you, man, it's imperative that I reach a regular Confederate Army unit without delay."

"Sure you do. You're one of their smartest officers. All the rebs wear these blue uniforms nowadays."

A guffaw of laughter rose from among the men, but the girl turned from where she had been stirring stew in a pot at the fire.

"He might be a Confederate spy, Ashley," she said, coming towards her leader.

For the first time Marsden gave his attention to the girl, for her voice came as a surprise. She did not speak in the coarse, strident tones of the usual cheap harridan one found among the irregular camp-followers. Nor did she have the tone of a rich, well-bred Southern belle. Her voice came somewhere between the two, like the daughters of small businessmen, storekeepers and the like Marsden met in the various Arkansas towns. The girl was bare-headed, her reddish brown hair hanging to just above her shoulders and curling out at the ends, showing signs of care not often seen among camp-followers. While not beautiful, she had an attractive face, one that might have looked merry and friendly in normal times but now had tight lips and cold, hostile brown eyes. The face was tanned by the elements, but showed no signs of being degraded by a life of debauchery. She stood about five foot six and the clothes she wore tended to reveal rather than hide her figure. A tartan man's shirt, a couple of sizes too large for her, still showed that she possessed a mature figure, while the levis pants she wore hinted at the rich curves and shapely legs underneath. High heeled riding boots almost completed the picture. No cheap, flashy jewellery spoiled her healthy, wholesome appearance, but a Tranter revolver was thrust into the left side of her waist band, its butt pointing inwards. Marsden formed an impression that the gun might be much more than a decoration.

Clearly Ashley respected the girl's opinion, for he turned towards her.

"Reckon he might, Jill?"

"He's riding alone," answered the girl. "Or we'd have heard from Thad by this time if there was more of them about."

"You could be right, gal," purred Ashley and turned to Marsden. "Are you a spy, feller?"

Marsden did not reply immediately, wanting time to think out his words. The man who had taken Marsden's watch stepped forward and drove his fist savagely into the young officer's belly, knifing the breath from his lungs and causing him to try to double over.

"You answer up when Ashley asks you something, boy!" the man warned.

"Keep back and leave him a chance!" snapped the girl called Jill. "He can't talk if you keep hitting him."

"Yeah?" began the man sullenly. "Well——"

"You pay Jill mind, Whit!" barked Ashley. "Stand back there and leave me do the questioning." Ignoring his man, Ashley looked to where Marsden, still firmly held, tried to rub the pain out of his stomach. "How about it, boy. Are you a spy?"

"You—You might say that," agreed Marsden hopefully.

His hope went crashing to the ground.

"Well, if you are," Ashley grinned, "I'll bet the Yankee Army'd pay right well to lay hands on you."

Marsden could have groaned at his mistake. The War meant only profit to men like Ashley, they were not moved by patriotic feelings. Mentioning that he might be a spy had been a wrong move, as Marsden now realised. It would have taken some time for Ashley's agent to make contact with the Zouaves and start the negotiations for the ransom and during that time a chance of escape could present itself. Far less time would be needed to contact any Union outfit with the view of selling a Confederate spy. The agent would not even need to locate a specific unit as in the case of a legitimate captive; in fact, if Marsden judged correctly, the agent probably knew exactly the right person to see when offering a prime piece of loot for sale.

"If he is a spy——" the girl put in, just a hint of worry creeping through her voice.

"The Yankees'll pay well enough to have him delivered," interrupted Ashley. "Or if they don't—well. I reckon his gear'll bring in something. He sure won't be needing it again."

A bellow of laughter greeted the remark, but Marsden noticed that the girl did not join in with her companions. Standing slightly behind the men, her eyes met Marsden's and an expression of doubt crept on to her face. The arrival of the man with Marsden's horse brought an end to further talk. A swarm of bushwhackers descended on the bay, eager hands grabbing out at the saddle-bags in search of loot. However the band retained some discipline, for the men holding Marsden did not relax their hold and a watchful hard-case with a rifle stood to one side ready to end any escape-bid.

After watching that nothing of real value escaped him, Ashley swung towards the men holding Marsden and snapped, "Clamp on those leg-irons in the Sibley and leave him safe."

The men holding Marsden knew their work and had sufficient strength to enforce their will on him. Swiftly they dragged him into the nearest Sibley tent, slung him to the ground and clamped on the leg-irons before he could make a move to prevent it. A pair of handcuffs followed, securing his wrists, the whole being coupled together by a chain long enough to allow him to sit up, but not stand erect. Marsden knew that kind of restraint, having seen it used on military prisoners, and was aware of the futility of trying to escape.

After securing Marsden, the men left the tent and he lay on the bare ground, as helpless as a chicken. Outside the flames leapt and flickered, showing against the tent's walls. Plates and cups rattled, talk and laughter reached Marsden's ears and he knew the men must be at their evening meal.

Time dragged by and at last the tent's flap raised. The girl entered, a plate of soup and mug of coffee in her hands. However, before coming within reach of Marsden's arms, she laid down the mug, took out her revolver and placed it in the doorway. Not until that had been completed did she advance and kneel by Marsden's side. Deftly she helped him into a sitting position and laid the plate on his lap.

"You'll have to make do with just a spoon, and there's no bread," she told him. "It's bear stew, that's all the meat we have. Thad downed a bear back on the bank of the Ouachita this afternoon."

"Look, Miss, you have to believe me," Marsden said in a low voice. "It's vital that I should reach a Confederate outfit. The lives of thousands of people depend on it."

"Are you a spy?"

For a moment Marsden thought of lying, although his upbringing and training revolted at the idea. He knew he could not make a lie that sounded like the truth and so shook his head.

"No. At least, not in the way you mean."

"Best eat that food while it's still warm," Jill said, her voice cold.

"You have to believe me——" groaned Marsden.

"Believe you?" spat out the girl. "Why should I believe anything you say? You're a Yankee and I'm David O. Dodd's sister."

Marsden knew the name and felt sick despair rising in

him, for he knew he could expect little sympathy from the sister of a man—a mere boy of seventeen—whom the Union Army executed as a spy shortly after their arrival in Little Rock. However, he determined to try.

"I'm no spy——"

"Nor was my brother. He was just a fool kid who thought he was a man. The information he gathered had no importance and he had no way of passing it to our troops even if it was important."

He had maps of our installations, the supply park——"

"I could expect a Yankee to excuse his kind," Jill snapped and started to rise.

"Listen to me, Miss Dodd!" Marsden put in, almost spilling the plate of stew as he tried to reach out and catch her arm. "Please listen!"

The girl had started to draw back, but something in Marsden's voice halted her and turned her eyes from the Tranter at the tent's door to his face once more.

"I'll listen, but I'm not saying I'll believe a word of it."

"I'm not denying that I'm a Union officer and that I'm loyal to the North. But I learned something important and I must tell it to a Confederate Army officer."

"What did you learn?" asked the girl.

"Two members of my regiment have a——"

Suddenly the girl swung her head towards the door, turned back to Marsden and said, "You start eating, mister."

Before Marsden could make a reply, the tent's flap lifted and Ashley peered in suspiciously.

"You're taking long enough, Jill," he said.

"Maybe you'd like to feed him," the girl answered.

"What was you talking about?"

"Feller reckons he has something real important to tell, something that might save a lot of our folks."

"Has, huh?" grunted Ashley. "What is it, Yankee?"

Marsden thought fast and knew that he must not speak of his knowledge to the bushwhacker. Not even the dreadful meaning of the scheme would change Ashley's attitude and knowing of it would give the bushwhacker something of saleable value. Maybe Ashley could evaluate the true worth, offered in the right place of Marsden's knowledge. Colonel Stedloe might pay well to have word of the scheme suppressed until after its successful completion and would not want too close an investigation into Marsden's desertion. Not, it would never do to let Ashley learn what brought him over the Ouachita.

"Come on, mister," the girl said. "Tell us about it."

"Well—It's—I—" Marsden forced himself to stutter and fumble like a man caught unaware or detected in a lie. "It's real important."

"I just bet it is," boomed Ashley. "So important that you reckoned Jill might set you free to slip away."

"You lousy, stinking *Yankee!*" Jill spat out, catching up the coffee mug and hurling its contents into Marsden's face.

While not boiling, the coffee proved hot enough to make Marsden rear up and tip over backwards. The plate of stew tipped from his knees and fell to the ground as he went. Jill turned and stormed out of the tent, scooping up her Tranter in passing and without a backward glance.

Bending down, a grinning Ashley helped Marsden sit up. "You shouldn't've tried that, soldier boy. Jill's a smart gal, but she could fall for a good-looking feller like you. Only she'd blow your head off as soon as look at you for wearing a Yankee uniform. Like to tell me what *did* bring you over here?"

"I'm on a scouting mission," answered Marsden, trying a bluff. It missed by a good country mile.

"In full dress and alone?" grinned Ashley. "Naw. I don't reckon so. You're on something important, just like you told Jill."

"Maybe I just got tired of fighting and want to surrender."

"Can't say as I go a lot on that, boy."

"You could find out by handing me over to the Confederate Army. After all, you are fighting on their side."

"Sure I am," replied Ashley. "Only I'm fighting for me. I don't give a damn whether they free the slaves or keep 'em as they are. Made good money before the War both running slaves to the North and setting 'em free, and sending 'em back to their owners for the reward. Only reason I support the South's so that if they win I'll be able to go on making money the old way."

"How do your men feel about that?'

"'Bout the same as me. They'd rather ride with me and make money than be in some army outfit."

"And Jill Dodd?"

A cold, warning scowl came to Ashley's face. "Jill hates you Yankees for what you did to her brother. If some reb regiment'd have her, she'd be wearing a grey uniform and fighting. Only they won't have a woman, so Jill rides with my outfit. She might have listened to you just now, but she won't any more. Anyways, I'm fetching Thad in and putting him to guard you. Thad's a mountain man, mighty sharp-eared; and he'll be told not to let anybody talk to you."

It seemed that Ashley did not entirely trust his female member. Anyway, he had no intention of allowing her to make further private conversation with his prisoner.

"How about some food?" asked Marsden.

"Jill's the cook, she might be mean enough to throw away what's left of the stew rather than have a Yankee eat it," Ashley answered. "Now why don't you tell me what brought you across the Ouachita. I'm going to learn one way or another when we get you back to our main camp, it'll be easier on your hide to talk friendly."

"I'm just a deserter," Marsden insisted.

Coming erect, Ashley shrugged. "It's your hide, boy. Only Thad's a mighty persuasive feller when he has to be. Think on it. Don't rush, you got all night."

CHAPTER THREE

Death of a Bushwhacker

Although he doubted if he would, Marsden slept at least some of the night. One of the bushwhackers brought him another plate of stew and mug of coffee soon after Ashley left, but the girl did not make another appearance. With the meal finished, Marsden was left to himself although the black silhouette on the tent's wall showed that Thad stood guard outside. Sheer exhaustion brought sleep to him at last, even though his chains forced him to adopt an uncomfortable position.

Dawn's grey light showed through the tent as Marsden opened his eyes. Outside, from what he could hear, the bushwhackers were awake and preparing to break camp. Voices and laughter reached his ears. Then the tent shook violently and began to collapse. The mass of canvas and central support pole came clattering down on him and he started to struggle, as well as he could in the chains, to extricate himself. Something round and hard prodded into his side, sending a wave of pain through him.

"Come on, Yankee!" whooped a voice. "Wriggle harder."

Marsden forced himself to lie still rather than give more cause for amusement to the men around the fallen tent. Outside, some half a dozen bushwhackers, including the man who felt Marsden's hard fist the previous night, gathered around. Raising his rifle, the man thrust it down hard at the mound which marked Marsden's position.

"Wriggle, Yankee!" whooped the man, as well as he could through his swollen lips. Again he thrust the rifle's muzzle down. "Come on, make a move to get—"

Suddenly the man felt a violent push which sent him staggering away from the tent. Jill Dodd, flush-faced and angry, glared at the others of the taunting group and pointed down with a quivering finger.

"Get that tent pulled off him!" she snapped.

"We was only funning, Jill gal," answered one of the men.

"Uncover him!"

"He's only a Yankee!" objected the man Jill pushed.

"He's a human being!" the girl answered hotly. "And he's going to be treated like one."

"There's some'd say you was going soft on that Yankee," stated the man. "Or maybe that you're forgetting what they did to your brother."

"I'm not forgetting anything!" Jill blazed back, the Tranter sliding into her hand. "If you want, I'll kill him right now. But if not, he'll be treated like a human being and not humiliated."

Slowly one of the men bent down, gripped the canvas and started to draw it from Marsden. Some of the others helped, uncovering the young lieutenant. Jill Dodd had a unique standing among Ashley's bushwhacker band. There had been other women who followed Ashley, but they were no more than cheap prostitutes who found making a living impossible due to the War and came to earn their keep with their bodies. Jill rode as a serving member of the band. Only once, soon after she joined them, had an attempt been made to treat her as a normal camp follower. The man who made the attempt died with a .36 Tranter ball in his belly and the remainder of the band took the hint. There were no further attempts on Jill's virtue. In the six months or so that she rode with the band, she proved herself able to handle a horse and shoot with the best of them and gained Ashley's confidence until he came to regard her as his second-in-command. None of the men around the tent doubted that Jill would shoot their prisoner, or that she meant to enforce her orders to them in the same manner if they disobeyed.

Always a late riser, Ashley appeared at the door of his tent and glowered across the camp.

"What's all the fuss?" he bellowed. "Why in hell haven't you started to break camp?"

Thad opened his mouth to answer, but the words did not come. Instead the man stared past his leader, made as if to raise his Perry carbine from the crook of his arm, thought better of it and stood still. His actions brought every eye towards the two uniformed figures who stepped from among the bushes and advanced towards the centre of the camp.

Clearly the new arrivals belonged to some crack Confederate regiment, for their uniforms, though travel stained, were of excellent material and cut. The taller of the pair, a gangling bean-pole who topped the six foot mark and had a miserable, careworn face, wore the usual kepi, cadet grey tunic—with a prominent Adam's apple showing through its stand-up collar—yellow-striped cavalry breeches tucked neatly into high-legged Jefferson boots. Instead of the usual weapon belt, he wore one of brown leather, broader and lower on the hips than normal, with a pair of walnut butted 1860 Army Colts in open-topped holsters, the holster bottoms secured to his legs by thongs. From the triple bars and arc of silk, denoting rank of sergeant-major, on his sleeves, that man must have more to his make-up than showed in his face and general manner.

Turning his eyes from the sergeant-major to the second

soldier, Marsden bit down an exclamation of surprise and hope.

On the face of it, the second man did not seem to be worthy of Marsden's interest. Even the term 'man' might be thought an over-statement when applied to a male person not long gone eighteen, and not large-grown for his age. Even with a white Confederate version of the Burnside hat—without one side turned up and devoid of a plume—on his dusty blond haired head, the second man clearly stood no more than five foot six. However, his shoulders had a width that hinted at strength and tapered down to a slim waist. Cool grey eyes looked from a tanned, handsome, intelligent young face, yet he did not give the impression of a swaggering half-pint who used his rank and social position to enforce his will on others. The uniform he wore set off his build, although it did not entirely conform with the Confederate Army's *Manual of Dress Regulations*. While the jacket had a stand-up collar, bearing the triple half inch wide, three inch long strips of gold braid of a captain, its wearer replaced the official black silk cravat with a tight rolled scarlet bandana. The double-breasted jacket bore the necessary double braid rank insignia on its sleeves and double row of seven buttons, but it ended at the waist, being without the prescribed 'skirt extending to halfway between hip and knee.' His riding breeches and boots had clearly been made to measure. Like his sergeant-major, the young captain wore a brown leather weapon belt, however, the two white handled Army Colts rode butt forward in their open-topped holsters and not so low hanging as the other man's.

"Release that man," ordered the small captain, the drawl in his voice confirming Marsden's thoughts of his place of origin even without the lieutenant needing a second look at the hat badge—a five-pointed star in a circle.

"He's our prisoner," Ashley replied, darting looks around him and seeing only the silent woods.

"He's an officer of the Union Army," stated the captain.

"I'll take him out of your hands."

Pleasure at his rescue was mingled with doubt and concern as Marsden turned his head in an effort to see what support the two soldiers had to enforce their demands. He saw nothing but the trees and bushes which surrounded the clearing. Surely the two men had not been fools enough to come unsupported?

Ashley seemed to think so. After another quick glance around, he started to raise a big right hand, meaning to grip the front of the small captain's non-regulation tunic.

"Just who do you reckon you are, you short——" Ashley began.

Out and up stabbed the captain's left hand in a move almost faster than the eye could follow. He caught Ashley's thumb neatly, his own thumb resting on the trapped member's second joint and fingers curling around, using leverage and counteracting pressure in a manner which threatened to snap the gripped bones. On securing his hold, the captain turned Ashley's palm upwards and at the same time raised the trapped hand. In an attempt to relieve the extreme pain caused by the hold, Ashley allowed his hand to bend inwards and twisted so he stood with his back to his captor. Moving a pace to the rear, but retaining his hold on the thumb, the captain raised his right leg, placed his foot against Ashley's rump and, releasing his grip, pushed hard. Ashley shot forward, stumbled, and went to his knees, mouthing a mixture of curses and orders to his men.

"Hold it right there!" ordered the sergeant-major, backing his words with a Colt in both hands.

The angry curses which rose from the bushwhackers died again. So interested had they been in watching Ashley's abortive attack on the captain that none saw the gangling non-com produce his weapons. However, all took in the sight of the lined Colts and discarded any ideas that might be forming on the matter of taking reprisals against the rash intruders.

Twisting around, still on his knees, Ashley studied the

situation. First to strike his notice was that the sergeant-major's full attention was fixed on his men. Next he observed that the captain had not as yet drawn his weapons.

"Which of you's Ashley?" asked the captain.

Already Ashley had one hand on the butt of his fancy Remington revolver. From the way he saw it, the two soldiers had made a deadly error in tactics. The moment that bean-pole non-com tried to turn his guns towards Ashley, the rest of the band would pump him. With a holstered gun, the captain could not draw, lift, aim and shoot before being swamped under. Satisfied on that point, Ashley jerked out his Remington and started to raise the gun shoulder high so he could take aim.

Instantly, even as Ashley started to pull his gun, the captain moved. Faster than the eye could follow, the left hand flashed across and closed upon the curved white grip of the right-side Colt. The moment the gun came clear of leather, its user's forefinger entered the triggerguard and already his thumb drew back the hammer. Nor did he take the time to lift the Colt shoulder high. His legs moved, halted to place him squarely facing Ashley, the knees slightly bent. Elbow almost touching his belt buckle, Colt no more than waist high, the captain fired his first shot. From first movement of the hand to crash of the shot took less than a second, but at the end of that time Ashley died with a .44 bullet in his head.

So swift had been the small captain's action that it took everybody in the clearing—with the possible exception of the lean sergeant-major—completely by surprise. Not for several years would Ned Buntline and his fellow writers publicise the speed with which some Western men could draw and shoot a gun. At the start of the War, Arkansas was so far past the frontier days that such superlative skill with weapons ceased to be a necessity of life and none of the bushwhackers knew just how fast and deadly a man raised in the West could be. Even Marsden, reared as he had been in New Mexico, felt surprised, for such speed and ability was the exception rather than the rule.

On the shot, almost before Ashley's body hit the ground, grey-clad soldiers dressed in the manner of the sergeant-major stepped from cover all around the camp. The guns held by the newcomers quelled any hope the bushwhackers might have had for avenging their leader's death.

Holstering his Colt, the captain pointed to Marsden and said, "Release him!"

The words jolted one of the bushwhackers into action. Taking out the necessary keys, he walked to Marsden's side and unlocked the handcuffs, then removed the leg irons. Slowly and stiffly, Marsden came to his feet. He stood working his arms and legs to get the stiffness out of them, touched his sore ribs and then rubbed his aching belly. All the time, he studied the bushwhackers. Finding the man he wanted, Marsden strolled over and held out his right hand.

"I'll have it back," he said.

"Sure, mister," gulped the man and reached for his inside pocket to take out Marsden's watch.

Taking the watch, Marsden slipped it back into its usual place. Then his left hand bunched into a fist and shot forward to drive into the man's stomach. Marsden struck hard, his fist sinking into the man's belly, doubling him over in a croaking mass of pain and dropping him to his knees.

"That's enough, mister!" barked the captain. "Take charge of the prisoner, Mr. Blaze."

A freckle-faced, pugnaciously handsome young lieutenant, his hat shoved back to show curly, unruly fiery-red hair, moved forward. While Mr. Blaze understood Marsden's feelings, and could guess that the Yankee lieutenant had been rough-handled by the bushwhackers, he also knew that the irregulars must be given no chance of grabbing a hostage.

"My apologies, sir," Marsden said, stepping away from

the bushwhackers and turning to the captain. "I was just exchanging gifts."

"Likely, mister," the captain answered dryly. "Take two men, Red, go with the lieutenant and collect all his gear."

"Yo!" answered the redhead and grinned at Marsden. "Just point it out and we'll get it back for you."

"That jasper there's wearing my weapon belt, most likely has my Colt in the holster, but I don't see my sword anywhere."

"Now don't you worry none about *them,*" smiled the redhead, but it was a cheery smile, not a malicious leer. "We'll take care of them for you."

Marsden nodded. For the moment he had almost forgotten that he was now a prisoner of war. "I expect so," he said, "Ashley there had my wallet."

After seeing Marsden started on his task of recovering the property looted from him, the captain gave his attention to the bushwhackers. Or rather Jill Dodd brought his attention to them by stepping forward and speaking.

"What about us?" she asked. "Why have you come here."

A momentary flicker of surprise crossed the captain's face as he heard Jill speak, but he made no comment about such a girl's presence among the bushwhackers.

"You all know that after Quantrill's raid on Lawrence, Kansas, the Confederate and Federal Governments outlawed unofficial raiding bands?" he said.

"General Chetley never objected before," Jill pointed out.

"General Chetley isn't in command any longer. By order of General Jackson Baines Hardin, all irregular groups are to disband, or join the regular forces and take service in the Army of the Confederate States."

"And if we don't?" snapped Jill.

"Also by order of General Hardin, any group continuing to stay in operation after warning by an officer of the Confederate Army will be treated as hostile and shot on sight."

"Damn it to hell!" Jill shouted. "We're fighting the Yankees too. Why only two weeks back we were over the Ouachita raiding their outposts."

"Sure," agreed the captain, his voice suddenly cold and grim. "You hit a couple of outposts and stirred up an area into which one of our patrols went to destroy an important supply depot. The Texas Light Cavalry lost some good men, and missed their chance through you. That's why I've been out with a patrol looking for Ashley."

"We didn't know," Jill gasped.

"And most likely wouldn't have cared either," growled the captain. "I found your main camp, burned it down."

"You did *what?*" hissed the girl.

"That's right, I burned it down. I found evidence there that Ashley had been trafficking in prisoners of war—and I also found property belonging to a group of Southern sympathisers who were attacked and robbed."

A look of shock came to Jill's face at the words. "That must have been when Ashley sent Thad, myself and six of the men on a scouting mission. I didn't know about the attack on our people. But I can't believe he would do such a thing."

"I can show you evidence," the captain told her. "There were four in the party killed. Two more badly wounded and the only woman wished that she had been killed."

"Is that why you shot Ashley?"

"I shot him to prevent him killing me, but knowing he was Ashley doesn't make me feel any worse. Now, ma'am, I'll get on with my business," said the captain, and he turned his attention to the watching bushwhackers. "All right, you have your choice, enlist in the army, or return to your homes."

"By cracky, cap'n," Thad said, stepping forward. "Fellers's can move as neat as your boys're worth siding. I'll come with you, if I can. Maybe you wouldn't've found it so easy to get our look-outs happen I'd been there instead of guarding the Yankee soldier-boy."

"Kiowa there'd've took you like the rest, *hombre,*" remarked the sergeant-major, indicating a tall, lean, Indian-dark sergeant, and speaking as if discussing the crack of doom.

"Drop it, Billy Jack," ordered the captain, "You'll ride with us when we leave, soldier. Any more of you?"

Feet scuffled and glances were exchanged, but none of the other bushwhacker males offered to give up their free life for the discipline and danger of fighting in a formal outfit.

"I'll go with you," Jill announced.

"We've no place for a woman, ma'am," smiled the captain. "If I was you, I'd go back home."

"Home?" Jill spat the word out as if it tasted bitter as bile. "My home is in Little Rock."

"Then come with me to Hope and I'll find you accommodation."

"Like hell! I'll make out on my own, thank you very much."

With that Jill turned and stamped angrily away. The captain watched her go, gave a sad shake of his head and swung back to the men.

"Collect your horses and gear, all of you!" he barked. "Remember this. If I see any of you in a bushwhacker band again, I'll order my men to shoot."

Turning, the captain walked over to where Marsden stood with Red Blaze. One of the bushwhackers looked at the sergeant-major and asked:

"Reckon he'd do it?"

"Mister," answered the lean non-com. "When Cap'n Fog says a thing, you'd best believe him, 'cause he sure as hell aims to do it."

"Is he *the* Cap'n Dusty Fog?" breathed the bushwhacker almost reverently.

"There's not two of 'em," admitted Sergeant-major Billy Jack miserably. "And you'd best get moving afore he decides to take you all in and find out who rode with Ashley when them Southern folks was killed."

"Captain Fog?" Marsden gasped, feeling foolish at repeating the small Texan's introduction, but unable to think of anything more adequate to say. "This is a pleasure and an honour, sir."

It was also, although Marsden did not mention the fact, the best piece of luck to come his way since he first heard of Castle and Silverman's plan.

Over the past year Captain Dustine Edward Marsden Fog's name had risen to prominence, until many folk ranked him equal to the great Colonel John Singleton Mosby as a fighting cavalry leader. Some even claimed that Dusty excelled Mosby in the art of light cavalry raiding. To the Union Army, Dusty Fog's name spelled serious trouble. At the head of his troop of the Texas Light Cavalry, he struck like lightning, caused havoc like a Texas twister, and disappeared like sun-melted snow only leaving more damage in his wake. Although only eighteen years old, Dusty had caused more than one Union veteran cavalry commander to wonder whether he knew his trade after all. Yet not only did Dusty Fog's name stand high as a raider, he was also a chivalrous enemy and no man need fear falling into his hands.

However, the latter consideration did not entirely account for Marsden's relief and pleasure at discovering his rescuer's identity.

"You'd better explain how a Union infantry lieutenant comes to be on this side of the Ouachita. Or did they take you on the other bank?"

Marsden smiled. No officer on fighting service would wear dress uniform, a point Dusty appeared to have noted already.

"I crossed the river to find you, sir," Marsden explained. "Well, not you exactly, but a Confederate outfit, preferably one from Texas."

"You'd best explain that, mister," Dusty said. "Only leave it until we're on the move. I don't think there'll be any more trouble from this bunch. And I want to get back to camp as soon as I can."

Ten minutes later the soldiers departed and the bushwhackers gathered in a disconsolate bunch.

"What do we do now?" asked one man.

Nobody appeared to have any suggestions until Jill moved forward. "Bury Ashley, then break camp," she ordered. "We'll strike west and cross the Texas line until this blows over. Then we'll start raiding again. Nobody's going to stop me fighting the Yankees."

CHAPTER FOUR

Marsden's Information

On leaving the bushwhackers' camp, Dusty and his troop escorted Marsden to the town of Hope by the shortest possible route. During the ride Marsden managed to convince Dusty of the importance of his business without going into details of Castle and Silverman's scheme. For his part, Dusty studied Marsden and assessed the other's character, deciding that such a man would not lightly become a deserter and traitor. So Dusty accepted the other's word and promised an immediate interview with General Ole Devil Hardin on their arrival at the regiment's headquarters.

The Texas Light Cavalry were encamped around the large, stately home of a wealthy Union supporter who fled when the flames of war grew in Arkansas. While riding through the smart, tented lines, Marsden found himself studying the excellent dress, equipment and spirits of the men. All appeared to be well-dressed and armed, also to be better fed than their Union opposites beyond the Ouachita. A party of men who passed Dusty's troop, each leading a packhorse loaded with deer and wapiti meat, gave Marsden an indication of the way the Texans fed. Southwest Arkansas might not be rugged frontier any more, but it still held vast herds of game; and should these fail the resources of Texas lay close at hand. Naturally the Confederate forces in Arkansas lived well.

Another reason for the well-being became apparent with a little thought. The Texas Light Cavalry might be a volunteer regiment, raised and financed by wealthy Texans, but its officers had seen combat before the War. A few served in the Texas War of Independence in 1836, others during the Mexican War of 1842, and most against either Indians, *Comancheros* or other Mexican bandits. So the officers possessed *practical* knowledge of fighting that few Eastern-bred volunteers had had a chance to gain. The rank and file of the regiment consisted of men who could ride and shoot almost as soon as they could walk, were trained and skilled in all the arts of cavalry warfare.

"Take over, Cousin Red," Dusty told his second-in-command on their arrival at the horse lines. "Unless you'd rather escort Mr. Marsden to see Uncle Devil."

"Who, *me?*" yelped Red Blaze, who tried to keep as far away from his uncle as possible. "No, sir, Cousin Dusty. I'll see the troop, *you* go visit Uncle Devil."

"Tell my striker to have Mr. Marsden's gear taken to our quarters, Red," Dusty ordered, handing his horse's reins to his guidon carrier. "This way, Mr. Marsden. We'll likely find the General at headquarters building."

A coloured servant took the two young officers' hats as they entered the big, Colonial-style white house. The servant had been in the former owner's employment but left behind when his master fled and took service with the new occupants.

"De General's in conference in de library, Cap'n Dusty, sah," the servant explained. "Got your pappy, Colonel Blaze and another colonel-gennelman with him." He rolled his eyes warningly. "If Ah was you-all, Ah'd steer clear of him, sah."

"I have to see him, Henry," Dusty replied.

"Well. Ah has done warned you, sah. Don't you say Ah didn't."

With that the negro turned and waddled away, shaking his head sadly in contemplation of the folly of the younger generation.

For all his brilliance as a cavalry leader, and abilities in other directions, Dusty hesitated a moment before raising his hand to knock on the library door. From inside the room, now converted to Ole Devil's office, came an angry bellow which Dusty knew all too well.

"But damn it to hell, John don't those foo—the General Staff back East realise I'm fighting a war here too? I'm not asking for much——" The voice died away as Dusty, sucking in a deep breath, knocked on the door, then resumed with, "Come in, damn it. Don't stand beating the door down."

"Mister," breathed Dusty, opening the door. "Your information had best be *real* important."

With that he ushered Marsden into a big, book-lined room. The four men at the desk in the centre of the room all looked at the new arrivals. Hondo Fog, senior major of the regiment, looking like an older and taller version of Dusty; bulky but iron hard Colonel Blaze; lean, ramrod straight, hawk-faced Ole Devil Hardin; the other colonel, a man of just over medium height, well-built, handsome, black haired and giving a hint of a cavalryman's build even though seated in a chair; all sat eyeing the two young officers coldly. Marsden only just held down a gasp as he recognised the younger colonel. That was the Grey Ghost, John Singleton Mosby himself. Yet Mosby mostly served farther east and should not be in Arkansas, unless——

"I'm in conference, Captain Fog!" growled Ole Devil scowling at his favourite nephew as if Dusty was a copperhead Southern supporter of the Union.

"Mr. Marsden requested an interview with you, sir," Dusty replied. "He says it's a matter of extreme urgency, sir."

The mention of Marsden's name drew all but Mosby's attention to the young Yankee. Giving a nod, Ole Devil told Marsden to come up and state his business.

"I hardly know where to begin, sir," Marsden said after marching smartly to the desk and throwing up a salute fresh from the pages of the drill manual.

"Try at the beginning, Mr. Marsden," Ole Devil suggested. "How did you come to be captured?"

"I found Mr. Marsden held prisoner at Ashley's camp, sir," Dusty put in.

"Which doesn't explain how he got there."

"The bushwhackers caught me while I was looking for a Confederate outfit to which I could surrender, sir."

Marsden saw a slight stir among the men, read added interest in their scrutiny and drew in a deep breath.

"Why did you want to surrender, mister?" asked Colonel Blaze.

"I learned of a plan to cause the withdrawal of most, if not all, of the Texas troops from the Army of the Confederate States, sir."

"And?" prompted Ole Devil.

"The plan calls for arming the Comanche, Kaddo and Kiowa tribes, sir."

"That plan was suggested two years ago, mister," Ole Devil said coldly. "I believe the idea was to supply the Indians with worn-out flintlocks in return for their assistance at fighting the Southern forces in Texas. It fell through when somebody pointed out that they wouldn't confine their activities to the Confederate Army, or even just to Southern sympathisers."

"This is a different plan, sir," Marsden insisted, marvelling a little at Ole Devil's knowledge of Union affairs. "The people putting it through——"

"Grant and Sherman would never authorise it," objected Ole Devil.

"They know nothing about it, sir. Nor will they until the plan is brought to a successful conclusion. Faced with a *fait accompli,* one resulting in the withdrawal of all Texas troops from the conflict, it would be hardly politic for even Generals Grant and Sherman to object."

Looking around the table, Marsden guessed he had made his point. Texas put some 68,500 men under arms in the Confederate forces, skilled fighting men. Its beef herds helped feed the South. Along its coast-line lay many ideal spots where blockade-running ships could land vitally needed supplies. If anybody made a plan which caused all that to be withdrawn from the Confederate cause, not even the two senior generals in the Union Army would dare to openly criticise the methods used by the plotters.

"And you think a few flintlocks will bring the three tribes together?" asked Dusty.

"Not flintlocks," Marsden answered. "Three hundred Sharps' breechloading rifles, ten thousand linen cartridge rounds—and the services of an Ager Coffee Mill gun."

"An Ager Coffee Mill gun?" repeated Dusty.

"Yes. It's a——"

"Mister, I know what it is," Dusty grunted.

Machine guns, repeating firearms, had long been a military dream and nightmare. A few types had made their appearance during the Civil War. The Confederate Army made use of the William Rapid Fire gun, an effective one-pounder repeating cannon. On the Union side, the Barnes and Ripley guns were tried, but the Ager Coffee Mill gun proved to be the only practical model—the Gatling not having made its debut at that date—and offered the Yankees a deadly addition to their armoury. Deadly, but not perfect, as Dusty pointed out.

"It's got its bad points, mister. If you fire it at over one hundred and twenty rounds a minute, it burns the barrel out."

Surprise at Dusty's knowledge prevented Marsden from remarking that the Confederate Army possessed no arm, not even the Williams gun, capable of equalling the Ager's rate of fire. Instead he said:

"Think of the effect such a gun would have upon men who know only weapons that need reloading after each shot."

"That's a good point, Mr. Marsden," Ole Devil stated and a low rumble of agreement echoed his words. "You mean that the men behind this scheme mean to present an Ager to the Indians?"

"Yes, sir, and instruct them in its use."

"How did you come to learn of this scheme, Mr. Marsden?" asked Hondo Fog.

Starting with his return from outpost duty, Marsden told the men everything about his discovery and decision to desert and bring word to the Confederate troops.

"Couldn't you have informed your own higher authority?" Mosby enquired.

"I doubt if General Thompson would object to it, sir," Marsden replied. "And it would take too long for word to reach General Sherman. You see, the plan has already been put into operation."

"When?" snapped Ole Devil, sitting forward in his chair.

"The wagon with the rifles and ammunition left eight days ago. The Ager was taken after them on the day before I returned from outpost duty. That was how I learned of the scheme. Castle is my company commander and when I came to report I heard he had left camp. So I started asking questions and learned what he was up to."

"And they can contact the Indians—without leaving their scalps on some coup-pole?" Ole Devil asked.

"They think so, sir. Castle and Silverman wouldn't willingly go into any danger. Their rendezvous with the arms wagon is where they meet a Union agent who trades with the Indians and can contact the old man chiefs of each tribe."

"His name?"

"I'm not sure, sir. The best I could learn was that they call him the Parson or something like that."

Suddenly Mosby thrust back his chair and came to his feet. He stepped around the desk, halting to face Marsden. Looking straight at the lieutenant's face, Mosby started a line of questioning the other expected.

"Just why are *you,* an officer of the Union Army, telling all this to us?"

None of the Texans spoke or offered to intervene. The same question had been in their heads, although possibly they could guess at the answer. However, Mosby, coming from Virginia—a state long past the days of Indian raids—might be able to make a more unbiased inquiry into Marsden's motives. Mosby had been a member of the Bar before the War and so knew how to question a suspect.

"I was raised in New Mexico, sir," Marsden replied. "I've seen Indian work."

An answer which could possibly have satisfied men who also knew the results of Indian warfare. Mosby did not appear to be convinced.

"Do you now expect General Hardin to make arrangements to quell this Indian uprising?"

"Yes, sir."

"By sending troops from his command to do it?"

"I hadn't thought of how he might handle the affair, sir."

"But if he does send, say a battalion, from the regiment, it might alter the balance of power in the Union's favour."

Marsden did not answer. All too well he knew how delicately balanced was the situation in Arkansas. Hardin's force numbered less than the Union troops and only their superior tactics and fighting ability prevented the Yankees from advancing and sweeping the state back under Federal control. The loss of even one battalion, acted upon by the Union forces, could see the Confederates pushed out of Arkansas.

"Well, Mr. Marsden?" demanded Mosby.

"I don't quite follow your question, sir," Marsden answered.

"Let me put a supposition before you, mister. Suppose this is a plot, not to arm and raise the Indians in Texas, but to create discord, uncertainty and alarm among the Texans in General Hardin's command?"

"If that had been my intention, sir," Marsden said hotly, "I'd have told Captain Fog of it in the presence of his men so that they could spread the word among the troops."

"Mr. Marsden," Ole Devil put in. "Do you give us your word that you are not trying to trick us in any way?"

"I do, sir."

Standing rigid at attention, Marsden met Ole Devil's frosty black eyes without any sign of flinching. He wanted to look at the others, try to read their thoughts, but knew that any attempt to do so might be construed as a sign of guilt. At last Ole Devil gave a nod and glanced at Mosby.

"One thing still puzzles me, Mr. Marsden," the Grey Ghost remarked, but much of the brusque note had left his voice. "This plan wasn't made during the past ten or so days. How come you didn't know of it earlier?"

"I'm a career soldier, sir. There's little common bond between us and the volunteer officers. They wouldn't let me in on anything of this nature in case I could offer concrete reasons why it would be ill-advised."

"Ill-advised!" Blaze snorted. "Arming the Indians would be rank lunacy."

"Just how did you learn of the scheme?" Mosby asked, ignoring the outburst.

"My suspicions were aroused, sir," Marsden answered and a faint grin came to his lips. "A bottle of whisky is a finer inducement to talking than torture, sir, properly used."

Mosby resumed his seat and looked around the circle of tanned Texas faces, with great attention to Ole Devil's expressionless mask. Taken with the news Mosby brought from the East, Marsden's information could be a terrible menace to the Confederate cause. It was Ole Devil's assumption of command that brought the Union advance in Arkansas to a halt, his leadership and tactics which held a superior force back beyond the Arkansas River. Through Ole Devil's actions, a large Federal army, badly needed elsewhere, must stay in Arkansas. With that knowledge in mind, Ole Devil requested reinforcements, one regiment each of infantry, cavalry and artillery, and Mosby had just brought word that the General Staff could not spare the men. Having seen, and heard, Ole Devil's receipt of the news, Mosby wondered how the other's feelings towards the Confederate States might be affected in the light of the new development. After all, Ole Devil *was* a Texan and of all the Southern states, Texas had the least interest in one of the basic causes of the War.

"Just how serious do you regard the situation, General?" asked Mosby when nobody offered to continue the conversation.

"It could be very serious," Ole Devil admitted.

"Maybe Kiowa could tell us what chance there is of the tribes merging, sir," Dusty put in. "He's lived among the Kiowa, his mother was one of them, and he'll maybe be able to help."

"Can he keep his mouth shut?" growled Ole Devil.

"If he says 'good morning' he's being real talkative, sir," grinned Dusty.

"Go get him then, Dustine. Take a seat, Mr. Marsden."

"Dusty!" Mosby put in as the small captain turned to leave. "While you're out, find my escort. Ask Sergeant Ysabel to report to me." He turned back to the desk. "Sam Ysabel knows the Comanche, married Chief Long Walker's daughter. He could know something."

"Sam Ysabel, huh?" grunted Colonel Blaze.

"Do you know him?" grinned Mosby.

"I've heard of him. Used to be a border smuggler. Ran a good line in duty-free Mexican wine—or so they tell me."

The latter part of the speech came as Blaze remembered

his pre-war post of justice of the peace in Rio Hondo County, and as such he should not be aware of the quality of a smuggler's goods.

"He's a damned good scout. Only one I have that's better is his son, Lon." Mosby remarked, ignoring Blaze's statement. "It's a pity the boy isn't here, but he went out with a patrol after a bunch of Yankees who caught and tortured a couple of our men."

On leaving the house. Dusty headed straight for the post sutler's building. He figured the conference had taken long enough for his troop to be dismissed and knew where to find the men he wanted. The sutler used one of the property's out-buildings and furnished it with a bar counter, tables and chairs gathered from unmentioned sources. Inside, a man could purchase such luxuries and necessities of life as the owner managed to gather, and generally relax from military discipline.

As Dusty expected, his sergeant-major and sergeant sat with a group of senior non-coms, one of them a man Dusty knew, but who did not belong to the Texas Light Cavalry.

"Gentlemen," Dusty greeted as he walked to the table. "My apologies. I'd like to see you outside, Billy Jack, Kiowa. You, too, Sergeant Ysabel."

Instantly the three men rose, although Sam Ysabel did not have a reputation for adhering strictly to discipline. Outside the sutler's store, Ysabel gave Dusty a broad and admiring grin.

"Billy Jack's just been telling me about what happened when you went over the Moshogen to give evidence at that Yankee shavetail's court martial,* sir," he said. "Haven't seen you since then."

"Billy Jack talks too much," Dusty answered. "You and Kiowa are wanted at the General's office."

"That means trouble," groaned Billy Jack. "You just see if it don't."

*Told in "The Fastest Gun in Texas."

"Likely," Dusty grinned for he was not fooled by his sergeant-major's pose. Under that lachrymose exterior lay a tough, capable and intelligent fighting man. "Go tell Cousin Red that we'll maybe pull out in a hurry."

"Yo!" replied Billy Jack and swung away from the others.

During the return to the house, Dusty took time to study the father of a man who would one day be his real good friend. At that time Dusty had not met Loncey Dalton Ysabel, better known as the Ysabel Kid, but had come into contact with the Kid's father once before.

Ysabel looked much the same; tall, well-built, powerful. Black-Irish and Kentuckian blood flowed through his veins, a fighting mixture without peer. He moved with a long, free stride, yet set his feet down lightly and in silence. An old Dragoon Colt hung at his right side, a James Black bowie rode his left hip in a Comanche medicine sheath. However, in time of war, unless Duty missed his guess, the Sharps breech-loading rifle would form Ysabel's chief defence and offence tool.

Neither of the sergeants asked any questions on their way to the house, and followed Dusty into Hardin's office. Inside, Dusty saw that time had not been wasted while he fetched the non-coms. Maps were spread out on the desk and the Confederate officers stood around it, while Marsden sat at one side, silent and obviously hiding his thoughts.

"Come in, gentlemen," Ole Devil told the non-coms. "Mr. Marsden, tell them what you told us about this scheme to arm the Indians."

Although he watched their faces as he talked, Marsden could see no sign of emotion, no hint at whether Ysabel or Kiowa believed him. Only once did either make any interruption. Following Marsden's mention of the Union agent who promised to gather the tribes, Ysabel asked:

"Would that feller's name be the Deacon, mister?"

"I——Yes, that's it. The man I was questioning didn't

talk too well when he reached that point and all I could make out was some kind of preacher."

"Know the Deacon, Hon—Major?" Ysabel asked of Dusty's father.

"Can't say I do." Hondo Fog had been local peace officer in the Rio Hondo before following Ole Devil to fight for the Confederacy.

"Naw. Most likely you wouldn't. He steered clear of places where the law was enforced. Was a trader, whisky, muskets, powder, lead, steel war-axes, he dealt in the lot."

"Could he arrange a meeting with the old man chiefs of each tribe, Sergeant?" asked Ole Devil.

For almost a minute Sam Ysabel did not reply. He exchanged glances with Kiowa, scratched his bristle-covered jaw and nodded.

"Sure, General," he answered quietly. "I reckon the Deacon could."

CHAPTER FIVE

They Have to be Stopped, Captain Fog

Silence fell on the room after Sam Ysabel's words, for none of the Texans doubted his knowledge of Indian affairs. Ysabel belonged to the hardy brotherhood who pushed into the wild, unexplored country with the desire to see what lay beyond the next hill. Unlike the settlers who followed in their wake, Ysabel's kind befriended the Indians, adopted their ways, learned their traditions and thoughts. Such a man could be expected to estimate the chances of Castle's scheme working with more accuracy than any settler. After a moment, Ysabel expanded on his statement.

"The Deacon knows enough of the old man chiefs to call all three tribes together, General. But he'd need some mighty strong medicine to make 'em listen to him."

"Three hundred rifles like your Sharps and ammunition would give him a good starting point," Ole Devil pointed out.

Ysabel looked down at his rifle. At that time the Model 1859 Sharps could claim to be the finest rifle in general use. Neither the Henry nor Spencer repeating rifles could equal its range, accuracy or dependability, and ammunition for both was difficult to obtain.

"Yes, sir," admitted Ysabel. "Spread out among the right folks in each tribe they'd gather a whole heap of support."

"Don't forget the Ager, sir," Dusty put in.

"I'm not likely to forget it, Captain Fog!" Ole Devil barked.

'You mean one of them Ager Coffee Mill guns, sir?" asked Kiowa.

"The men behind this scheme are taking one to the meeting and intend to offer it as support to the raiding parties," Ole Devil replied.

"What would its effect be, Sam?" Mosby enquired.

"Big medicine, Colonel," Ysabel answered soberly. "Just about as big as you could get. They'd think it was a Devil Gun. I tell you, one good victory with that thing backing 'em and those Yankees'd have every Indian in the whole damned state painting for war."

"As bad as that?" asked Blaze.

"Worse," grunted Ysabel. "Even such of the old man chiefs who wanted to stay out of it wouldn't have any say with that thing siding the war-shouters."

"We have to stop the Ager falling into Indian hands, sir," Dusty stated.

"Yes, they have to be stopped, Captain Fog," agreed Mosby. "The question is how do you stop them."

"Prevent them from contacting the Indians," Dusty suggested.

"To do that, you have to find them," Blaze pointed out. "Did you learn either their rendezvous, or the meeting place with the Indians, Mr. Marsden?"

"No, sir. The informant collapsed into a drunken stupor before I learned either. Each party slipped through the Ouachita Mountains, avoiding your patrols, and were to meet somewhere on the Red River."

"There're a hundred crossing points on the Red," Hondo

growled. "We can't cover them all. And Texas's a whole heap too much land for us to start combing it to find a small party."

"What escort did the two parties have, Mr. Marsden?" asked Ole Devil.

"One mounted company of Zouaves were taking the wagon to the rendezvous, but the Deacon claimed he could handle the situation better without so many men and so the escort was to return when the meeting was made."

"Why send them separately, Mr. Marsden?" Blaze put in.

"The Ager hadn't arrived and a messenger from the Deacon arrived with news that he was expecting representatives from each tribe to visit him. He wanted something to show the Indians when they arrived. So it was decided to send off the arms wagon immediately. Castle and Silverman, in civilian clothing, were to follow with the Ager on a light artillery mount. They had a guide to take them through your lines."

Ole Devil might have commented that lack of men prevented him from making accurate coverage of the Ouachita Mountains, but did not bother. Nor did Mosby need any explanation, for he specialised in slipping through the enemy's lines and knew how it could be done, especially in mountainous land.

"It doesn't help us much to know where the rendezvous might be," the General commented. "They'll have passed that point now."

"Just thought of something, General," Ysabel said. "A thing like this, getting the three tribes together I mean, calls for a special medicine place. You don't just ask Comanche, Kiowa and Kaddoes to meet up and forget all the years of war in any old place."

"Sam's right, General," Kiowa agreed. "It has to be some place that the Great Spirit keeps for his-self."

"Kind of sacred ground,' continued Ysabel. "All the tribes have them. Places where enemies can meet and talk things out without needing to watch for sneaky games. A medicine place'd be the only location you could gather Comanche, Kiowa and Kaddo without getting trouble."

"Where would such a place be?" asked Ole Devil.

"Can think of half a dozen scattered about Texas," Ysabel replied. "There's one on the Sweetwater, another on the Colorado."

"They'd be too far south," Dusty guessed, consulting the maps. "The Yankees need something close at hand."

"How about the joining of the Salt and Clear Forks of the Brazos?" Kiowa put in. "That's an old medicine place."

"I reckon you hit it, Kiowa," Ysabel enthused, looking at the spot to which the lean sergeant pointed. "The Deacon knows that country pretty well."

"It's a touch close to Fort Worth and Dallas," objected Ole Devil.

"Over a hundred miles from the nearest, and Indian country at that," Ysabel replied. "No, sir. Was I asked, I'd say that's our place."

Once again all the men gathered around and studied the maps. To experienced soldiers, the true meaning of the insignificant spaces upon the paper stood plain and clear. A thumb and forefinger might span from the Red River to the fork of the two tributaries of the Brazos, but all knew how many actual miles lay between the points.

"With four days lead, they'll be over the Red now," Hondo pointed out. "But with wagons they'll be travelling slow. We might send a battalion——"

"I can't even spare a company, not and hold out here in Arkansas," Ole Devil answered. "And a company would travel too slowly to intercept them."

"A small party could move fast enough, sir," Dusty put in.

"How small?" asked Ole Devil.

"I thought myself, Kiowa, Billy Jack and two more would do," Dusty said. "A party that size, mounted on the pick of our horses, could cover between thirty and forty miles a day even without taking remounts from any Confederate outfit we happened across."

"It's getting on for three hundred miles to that fork, Dusty," Hondo warned.

"Yes, sir, but if we're lucky we'll catch the Yankees before they reach it. How many men'll be with the wagons, six, ten, a dozen at most. The Indians wouldn't stand for many more than that. With surprise at our back, I reckon we can handle them."

Ole Devil sat back in his chair, the impassive mask dropping on to his face and warning all who knew him that he was thinking. Every man present understood the problem facing the grim-faced General. His orders were to prevent further Union advance in Arkansas, and if possible regain the territory already taken. While he could hold the Yankees beyond the Arkansas River and prevent their gaining more land, he needed every man to do so. Despite Dusty's youth, he was a valuable fighting leader and a man not easily spared. To let Dusty go, even with only four men, would seriously weaken Ole Devil's precarious hold on the delicately balanced position. Yet to refuse would be just as disastrous. Once the Indians took to the warpath, there would be no stopping them short of using considerable force. Nor would the blood-crazy, coup-seeking braves differentiate between soldier and civilian, or between man, woman and child. The Indians, would ravage Texas from north to south, leaving the country, already weakened by the number of men away at the War, a burning, bloody ruin. Ole Devil knew the result of such an Indian uprising and also realised that every Texan serving the Confederate Government would want to return home to defend, or avenge, his family once the news spread.

So Ole Devil had to balance the temporary loss of a good officer against the possibility of the South losing thousands of badly needed soldiers. There could only be one answer.

"Who do you want with you, Dustine?" he asked. "And

before you say it, I can't let Mr. Blaze go with you. I need one of you to lead your troop."

"You'd best take Sergeant Ysabel, Dusty," Mosby put in. "He knows the country——"

"And I'm kin to Long Walker, top war chief of the Comanche," Ysabel finished for his commanding officer. "It's a pity Lon's not here, Long Walker's his grandpappy."

Like many of his kind, Sam Ysabel had taken an Indian wife; unlike some of the frontiersmen, he remained true to the Indian girl and grief at her death sent him from the Comanches, although he stayed in touch with them.

"Be pleased to have you, Sergeant," Dusty said. "And for the other man——"

"May I be the other man, sir?" Marsden put in.

All the Confederates in the room looked at the young Union officer. He read a mixture of surprise, inquiry, suspicion even in the various faces.

"Why, mister?" asked Ole Devil.

"My people are causing the trouble, sir. I'd like to help put it right."

"If you fall into Union hands, you'll be shot, boy," warned the grim-faced General, but an almost gentle note crept into his voice.

"I will whether I see it through or stay here, sir, in the end." A man who acted as Marsden had could expect death at the hands of his own people. He knew and accepted that fact before he started out for the Ouachita. However, he wanted to see through the thing he started. Knowing the risks they took, he stood a fair chance of never coming back and preferred that to bringing shame upon his family.

Dusty smiled. "We'll be travelling light, real light, sir. Mr. Marsden's an infantry officer, does he think he can stand the pace?"

"I trained for cavalry almost from birth, sir," Marsden answered.

"Then you can come along," Dusty promised. "With your permission, sir, I'll start making my preparations.

We'll pull out at first light in the morning."

Although they might be able to leave earlier, Dusty knew it would be better to utilise the rest of the day in making sure they had the best horses and preparing for the long, hard ride ahead.

After Dusty's party left the room, Mosby turned to Ole Devil. "Do you think we can trust Marsden, sir?"

"I know we can," Ole Devil answered. "Haven't seen the boy since he was ten, but he's his father's son."

"How about it, Dustine?" queried Ole Devil.

"You know his family, sir?"

"You might say that, Colonel Mosby. I served with his father in the Mexican War. General Marsden is Dustine's god-father and young Marsden there is my god-son. They named him Jackson Hardin for me. Now, gentlemen, we'll see what we can do to get my god-son out of the mess he's in. You're a pretty good lawyer, John. Is there a precedent for his action?"

"If there is," Mosby replied after a moment's thought, "I can't think of it."

"Or me," admitted Ole Devil. "I think that we'll have to try direct methods. Hondo, can you take down a letter to General Philo Handiman, we'll send it under flag of truce to the nearest regular Yankee outfit, they'll pass it on to Philo in Washington."

Not knowing that his future was under consideration, Marsden resigned himself to his fate. In an attempt to stop himself thinking of his ruined career and possible fate, he studied the scenes around him. First thing to strike his eye was that the Texas Light Cavalry's camp showed none of the casual slovenliness he associated with volunteer outfits. Next of interest being the amount of Union Army gear on view. Tents, leatherwork, arms all bore the mark of Union make, even though the voices around the camp sounded Texan.

"You look surprised that we're living so well, mister," Dusty remarked.

"I am, sir," admitted Marsden.

"We couldn't do it relying on our own folks' supplies. Apart from the uniforms, we mostly draw on the Yankees for anything we need."

A faint smile came to Marsden's lips at the small captain's words. Something told Marsden that the forthcoming trip would be an education for him and that he might gain knowledge of use in his career. The smile went as Marsden realised that in all probability he no longer had a career or a future.

Telling the two sergeants to grab a meal, then report to his tent and bring Billy Jack, Dusty took Marsden to his quarters in the officers' lines. Another of Marsden's illusions went as he found that the wedge tents had been stockaded and gave every hint of permanency.

"We aren't going anywhere," Dusty remarked in answer to the other's comment on the permanent nature of the quarters. "Not unless it's back over the Arkansas."

The tent proved to be spacious, although not luxuriously furnished. However, it compared favourably with Marsden's quarters with the Zouaves. Dusty shared the tent with his second-in-command and Red Blaze sat on one of the beds, his jacket off, Marsden's weapon belt lying next to his own. A pair of saddles rested on burros, wooden racks like inverted A-shapes. One glance told Marsden that the Texans might use many Union items, but they stuck to their range rigs. The saddles had double girths and the type of low horn only rarely seen in New Mexico. A coiled, thirty-foot rope hung on one side of each saddle's horn, with the slings for carrying a sabre at the other side. From the saddles, Marsden turned his attention to the arms leaning against the burros. As the Spencer carbine did not come into use until after the War started, he concluded the pair in the tent must be battlefield captures.

From the Spencers, Marsden turned his eyes to the sabres and saw something that interested him. He wondered how he could satisfy his curiosity.

"Everything all right, Dusty?" Red asked.

"Sure. Have a bed brought in for Mr. Marsden, he's our guest."

The order aroused no comment from Red. Among the regular officers of the Union and most of the Confederate brass the rules and chivalries of war were still honoured. A captured officer could expect decent treatment and certain privileges.

"I'll tend to it," Red promised. "His weapons are here, I left them until you told me how to dispose of them."

"You can let him have them back. He'll be riding out with me in the morning."

Once again Red refrained from asking questions, although he clearly showed his surprise. Never before had Dusty taken a captive to a prisoner-of-war camp, his time being too fully occupied for him to be spared on such an unimportant detail. Nor did the return of the weapons lessen Red's perplexity. While a regular Union officer's sword might be returned to him by his captors, no Confederate would willingly part with such a highly-prized item as an 1860 Army Colt; the most highly thought-of handgun to have made its appearance in the War.

At last Red could hold his curiosity no longer. "What's on, Cousin Dusty?"

"I've a chore to handle, Mr. Marsden's going along."

"Taking the troop?"

"Nope. Just Billy Jack and Kiowa."

"Can you tell me about it?"

"Later maybe," Dusty replied. "Have you ate yet?"

"No, thought I'd wait for you."

"As soon as we've washed up, we'll go and grab a meal then. Care to take first crack at the wash-bowl, Mr. Marsden."

"Thank you, sir," Marsden replied.

"I'll go tell the striker to bring more water," Red said, rising and walking from the tent.

Restlessness drove Marsden to make conversation and

he sought for something to talk about.

"That's not regulations, is it, sir?" he asked, indicating the jacket Dusty removed and placed on the second bed.

A grin came to Dusty's face. "A shavetail called Mark Counter, in Sheldon's outfit, started the no-skirt jacket and the idea caught on. I find it better for work than the authorised undress uniform."

Then Marsden recalled the thing which interested him on his arrival. Crossing the tent, he looked at the sabre on one of the burros.

"May I, sir?" he asked, reaching towards it.

"Feel free," Dusty replied.

At West Point and since, Marsden had always heard that the Confederate Army possessed poor swords. Shortage of material due to the blockade of Southern ports, lack of skilled tradesmen and forging facilities prevented the rebels from owning decent weapons. However, the pair of swords in that tent showed excellent workmanship and proved to be of Southern manufacture; no Union company would use the letters C.S.A. in the hilt pattern of its produce.

The sabre Marsden examined had sharkskin covered grips secured with gilt wire, and its blade sported a stopped blood gutter and an additional thin, deep channelling on both upper sides of the blade for added flexibility and strength. On examination, Marsden found the blade's steel to be as good as any from the Union force. He hefted the sabre, noting its razor-sharp edge, and found he did not care for its balance.

"A fine blade, sir," he said, returning the sabre to its sheath.

"The Haiman Brothers made it for me," Dusty replied. "A thirty-two inch blade instead of thirty-six, and a shade lighter than the artillery sabre."

Now it had been pointed out to him, Marsden saw the difference in length between the two sabres.

"Do you find yourselves at any disadvantage using it against arms of the conventional length, sir?" he asked, and regretted the question as soon as the word left his mouth. A small man in a large man's world might resent any comment or hint at his lack of size.

"Nope," Dusty replied with a grin. "It only means that I have to get closer to the other feller than he gets to me."

Apparently Dusty took no offense. Suddenly Marsden realised that Dusty Fog accepted his lack of inches and, very sensibly, made no attempt to carry the full-length cavalry sabre in an effort to hide his small size. Looking first at the sabre, then at Dusty, Marsden wondered how well the small Texan could handle the weapon. Before he could go into the matter, Marsden saw Dusty's striker, a cheery young Negro, arrive with water.

"All right, mister," Dusty said. "Let's wash, go have a meal, then we'll get everything ready for pulling out in the morning."

CHAPTER SIX

Mr. Marsden Picks A Horse

"Like I said," groaned Billy Jack as Dusty finished telling him of their latest assignment, "trouble."

"Sure," agreed Dusty. "We'll need the pick of the horses. I want a real good mount for Mr. Marsden."

The mournful pose left Billy Jack and he nodded, then continued with his preparations.

"Carbines?" he asked.

During his meal at the officers' mess Dusty had given some thought to the matter of armament. On such a ride every ounce of weight counted and he balanced the value of taking along carbines and ammunition (giving his party weapons with a longer range than their Colts) against the extra loading of the horses.

"Just sidearms," he answered. "We're not fighting unless we're forced. Fifty cartridges, powder flask and twenty round ball per man."

"Huh, huh," grunted Billy Jack. "Pack hosses?"

"Two, carry food for the mounts and jerked meat. We're travelling light."

"Like to take my old rifle along, Cap'n," Ysabel put in.

Dusty studied the big Sharps for a moment. Men like Ysabel felt lost without a rifle handy, regarding it almost as a part of their own body. Knowing the independent nature of Ysabel's kind, Dusty took the request as quite a compliment. Not that he intended to allow that to sway him in any way. His party might find use for a rifle and Ysabel was the best man to handle it.

"Take it, Sergeant," he authorised. "No more than fifty rounds though."

"Yep," agreed Ysabel. "Won't need no cartridges for my belt gun. I allus use loose powder and round ball."

"I'll leave it to you," Dusty answered.

"Jerked meat, coffee, sugar do for food?" asked Kiowa.

"That and anything we can pick up on the way," Dusty replied.

Watching the others, Marsden realised that all knew their business and had ridden on many missions of a dangerous nature. The questions and orders were merely routine, for each man knew his part.

"Let's go and see about your horse, Mr. Marsden,"Dusty suggested. "Billy Jack, head down and tell Sergeant Granger I want him to put the remuda in the big corral."

"Yo!" replied the gangling non-com and was about to depart when Dusty joined him and said something in a voice too low for the others to catch. "I'll tend to it, Cap'n Dusty."

"Leave the food side to you, Kiowa," Dusty went on and the sergeant left on Billy Jack's heels.

"Need me for anything, Cap'n?" asked Ysabel.

"Come down to the corral with us," Dusty suggested. "If you're ready, Mr. Marsden, we'll go see about collecting your horse."

Although not a member of the party, Red Blaze had been present. He rose from his bed and prepared to carry on with his duty of escort to Marsden. Knowing that the Union possessed a reasonably efficient spy network even in

Arkansas, Dusty took no chances of news of his mission leaking out. While in camp Marsden would be treated as a prisoner-of-war and kept under escort. Dusty knew he could rely on his cousin to keep quiet about the mission and so asked Red to be Marsden's escort even though the redhead held a higher grade of rank than the prisoner.

Dusty did not appear to be in any great rush to reach the corral. Strolling leisurely through the camp, he and Red kept up a friendly conversation with Marsden and did nothing to prevent the Union officer from examining his surroundings. At last they reached the horse lines. All around them, the never-ending business of cavalry soldiers went on. Men cleaned up the picket lines, led horses to water, saw to feeding their mounts. To a casual, inexperienced observer everything might have seemed to be in wild confusion, but Marsden saw the disciplined purposefulness of the scene. One thing he noticed was that the officers and sergeants clearly trusted their men to carry out the assigned work without constant supervision. That was understandable. Born in a land where a horse was far more than a means of transport, being an absolute necessity of life, the men of the Texas Light Cavalry knew better than neglect their mounts.

Never had Marsden seen such a fine collection of animals. Nor did his admiration decline when he approached one of a series of big pole corrals. Already a number of horses had been driven into the corral and, although they belonged to the regiment's reserve of mounts, Marsden noticed their glossy coats and general signs of good health.

"Take your pick," offered Dusty.

Sensing a test of his horse-knowledge and judgment, Marsden swung himself up to sit on the top rail. Once there he started to examine the horses with careful eyes and knew straight off that no easy task lay before him. All the horses showed well-rounded frames that told of perfect condition and looked as hard as exercise and training could make them.

At last Marsden saw what he wanted. While not the biggest horse in the corral, he decided to ask for the sorrel gelding with the white star on its face. Everything about the sorrel pleased him. Its head gave an impression of leanness, although with good width between the eyes, which were set well out at the side and promised a wide range of vision; depth through the jaw, the lips clasped firmly over the teeth and the nostrils flaring well open. That head insured good breathing capability while the erect ears pointed to alertness. Of course, Marsden knew the old dealers' claim that one did not ride the head; but a good head, all things being equal, usually meant a good horse. The sorrel's neck had sufficient length and strength to give a good carriage to the head. A short back, level from the dip behind the withers and a well ribbed-up frame offered a firm base for the saddle, while the powerful loins, fore-limbs and legs hinted at power, stamina, speed and agility.

Several of the horses showed up almost as well, but the sorrel possessed an undefinable something which made Marsden select it.

"I'll take that one," he said, indicating the horse.

Almost before the words left Marsden's mouth, Billy Jack swung up alongside him. The sergeant-major held a sixty foot long Manila rope in his hands, a running loop dangling ready. Up and out whirled the loop, flying through the air to drop around the sorrel's neck. The throw had been so swiftly and neatly made that Marsden turned towards Dusty meaning to comment on it. A smile played on Dusty's lips, mirrored on the faces of Red and Billy Jack. Suddenly Marsden knew that the sorrel was placed among the other horses, on Dusty's whispered orders, as a test of his knowledge.

A momentary irritation rose in Marsden's thoughts. In addition to being at least three years older than Dusty Fog, he had attended West Point and was not just some volunteer who held rank because his uncle happened to be the commanding general. Then sober thought wiped out the irritation. Dusty was embarking upon a desperate and dangerous assignment, also upon a very long and arduous journey. One could not blame him for taking no chances.

"That's a good horse, mister," Billy Jack remarked, drawing in on his rope. "Only I wouldn't let the Yankee General, Custer, catch you riding it."

"Why?" Marsden asked, watching the calm way the sorrel accepted the rope.

"It used to belong to him."

Then Marsden remembered that among his other exploits Dusty had led a raid on the 7th Cavalry's camp and drove off a fair number of the regiment's mounts. Knowing something of Custer's taste in horses, Marsden decided that possibly the sorrel had been one of the General's personal mounts.

"Reckon you'd best use one of our saddles, Mr. Marsden," Dusty suggested as Billy Jack led the sorrel form the corral.

"Had one fetched down for you, mister," Billy Jack called over his shoulder. "It's there on the rail."

Sensing something out of the ordinary in the air, a small knot of soldiers hovered in the background. On seeing that Marsden went towards the rail-hung saddle, an air of anticipation ran through the watching men. All wanted to see what kind of a horseman the Yankee shavetail might be. With his army's reputation to uphold, Marsden hoped that he might put on a good display. However, he had never used a double-cinched range saddle and wondered if he could handle it correctly.

"Here, Yankee," a voice said. "I'll lend you a hand."

Turning his head, Marsden looked towards the speaker. All in all the approaching man did not strike Marsden as being the type to voluntarily offer assistance. He was a tall, burly young man with a sullen truculent face and wore the uniform of Mosby's Rangers. However, Marsden knew that appearance could be deceptive and so raised no protest. Not that the soldier intended to burden himself to any great extent, for he took the blanket and left Marsden to handle the saddle. Not that Marsden objected, as he liked to saddle his own horse.

Walking to the sorrel, the soldier went around it, halting on the side away from Billy Jack and in a position that hid him from the watching men. he took his time in getting the blanket into place, slipped a hand under it to ensure its smooth, unwrinkled fit, then let Marsden swing on the saddle. To one side of the group, Sam Ysabel glanced at the horse then turned his eyes to study Marsden's helper.

While saddling the sorrel, Marsden took the opportunity to study the animal. It showed no objections at receiving the saddle, although it moved restlessly when he first put the rig on. Clearly the sorrel was used to being saddled and ridden, however it might want to debate the matter of who ran things when it felt Marsden's weight for the first time. Not that Marsden felt worried, he reckoned he could hold his own in that kind of company.

With everything set, Marsden gripped the saddlehorn, placed a foot in the stirrup iron and swung upwards. Cocking his leg over, Marsden settled his weight down in the saddle. Instantly the sorrel gave a shrill scream of pain and took off in a wild leap. Only by a grab at the horn did Marsden prevent himself from being thrown. He came down hard on the saddle once more after being raised clear out of it, landing just as the horse's feet touched the ground again. Another scream of pain burst from the horse and it took off once more. Marsden could not imagine what was happening. He did not for a moment believe that Dusty misled him or gave him an outlaw horse. No horse could have fooled Marsden so completely as to its character. Yet the sorrel seemed to be almost crazy as it bounded and leapt, squealing on each leap's completion.

Dusty threw a glance at the burly soldier who helped Marsden, then turned and raced to where a saddled horse stood ready for use in an emergency—a simple precaution when handling spirited animals that might be snuffy through lack of work. Taking off in a bound, Dusty leap-frogged over the horse's rump, landed in the saddle, caught up the reins and started the animal moving. A second rider, a man returning from some duty, sent his mount racing towards the wildly leaping sorrel so as to give assistance.

Bringing his horse alongside the sorrel, Dusty yelled a warning to Marsden and hoped the other knew what to do. Marsden still stuck on the horse despite his amazement at its behaviour. True he expected some trouble, but nothing so serious as the wild fit of bucking. He knew that somehow each time he slammed down into the saddle, the impact brought on another spasm. Yet there was no way he could dismount short of leaping clear and chancing a broken leg. Then he heard Dusty's yell and saw the small captain loom alongside, coming in very close. At the same moment a second rider appeared at the other side, crowding in on the sorrel.

"Now!" Dusty yelled as he extended an arm towards Marsden.

Grabbing out, Marsden hooked an arm around Dusty's shoulders and felt the Texan's hand clamp hold of his belt. Then he kicked his feet free of the stirrups and felt himself dragging over the saddle. A moment later he hung suspended from Dusty and the sorrel drew away from them still bucking. Leaning from his saddle, the second rider managed to catch the sorrel's trailing reins and brought the animal to a halt.

Once clear of the sorrel, Dusty set Marsden down on the ground. Swinging from his saddle, Dusty left the horse to its own devices and strode towards where the sorrel stood fighting its reins. Dusty took the reins and started to calm the horse, speaking gently and holding its head down. Hearing a burst of laughter, Dusty threw a cold, ominous glare at the Mosby man who had helped Marsden.

When the sorrel calmed down and stood still, although

shivering, Dusty moved alongside it and started to loosen the saddlegirths. Running forward, Marsden helped to strip off the saddle. With an angry gesture Dusty reached under the blanket and brought something out. Marsden looked down at a small iron ball with four knobbly lumps of pyramid-shape rising from it.

"So that's what made him buck!" Marsden breathed. "But I don't——"

"I do!" Dusty growled and swung from Marsden to walk to where the burly Mosby man stood wiping his eyes and still laughing. "Did you put this under the sorrel's saddle blanket?"

With an effort the soldier stopped laughing and the truculence returned to his sullen features. "Sure I did. Figured to see how well the Yankee shavetail could ride a hoss."

Which, as any member of the Texas Light Cavalry could have warned the soldier, was most definitely not the manner to use when answering a very annoyed Captain Dusty Fog.

"Damn you, Heimer!" Sam Ysabel bellowed. "I'll——"

"I'm handling this, sergeant!" Dusty cut in.

It had long been Heimer's boast that he showed respect only for Colonel Mosby and he objected to having a short-growed kid-officer from another regiment mean-mouthing him.

"So I shook the shavetail up," he scoffed. "Hell, he's only a Yankee——"

"Walk that horse until it cools down," Dusty ordered quietly.

"Like he——"

Heimer's words chopped off abruptly as Dusty moved forward to insist on obedience to orders. Out and up drove Dusty's left fist, sinking with some force into the pit of the unsuspecting Heimer's stomach. Knowing his own size and reputation as a rough-house brawler, Heimer never thought the small captain dare lay a hand on him. So the blow, anything but a light one, took him completely by surprise.

Grunting, he went back on his heels, took a pace to the rear and doubled over. Dusty whipped up his other hand, swinging it around so that the knuckles caught the offered jaw with a crisp thud.

Lifted erect by the punch, Heimer staggered back several feet before he managed to catch his balance and come to a halt. Then he gave an enraged bellow, lowered his head and launched a charge calculated to flatten a much larger man than the grim-faced officer who so rough-handled him.

"We'd better stop him!" Marsden gasped and started to move forward.

"Leave be, Jack," answered Red Blaze, clamping hold of the other's arm and restraining him. "Dusty won't hurt that feller none."

At which point Marsden began to see that his fears had been misplaced.

Instead of sidestepping the other's rush, Dusty waited for it. However, before Heimer struck him, Dusty's hands shot out and clamped hold of Heimer's jacket just below the armpits, arms locking against the man's bent-forward body and holding it. Moving fast, Dusty pivoted his hips slightly to the left and started to fall backwards. Suddenly Dusty hooked his right foot behind Heimer's left leg and pressed his left boot against the front of the other's right ankle. Heimer howled as his feet lost all control. By using Heimer's momentum, Dusty changed the charge into a head-long tumble. While a good horseman, Heimer did not have time to break his fall. He felt himself falling, let out a wail and landed with a crash upon his back.

Bounding up, Dusty went forward, bent and laid hold of Heimer's jacket front. With a heave, Dusty fetched the winded man to his feet and then heaved him into Sam Ysabel's waiting arms.

"See he tends to the sorrel, Sergeant!" Dusty barked. "And if it isn't fit for use in the morning I'll stuff his pants with these damned burrs and ride him on a cannon until he wishes his mother and father never met the one time they did."

Gripping Heimer by the scruff of the neck, Ysabel shook him savagely. "You hear that, boy?" he growled. "Well, you'd better believe it. Happen that hoss ain't fit to be rid, Cap'n Fog'll surely do what he says."

While he claimed to be tough, and could not be counted among the world's brighter intellects, Heimer knew enough to call a game quits. He did not know how the small captain managed to handle him with such comparative ease, but his every instinct warned him that Dusty could most likely repeat the process, or maybe even find a rougher and more painful method next time. Nor did he offer to raise objections to Sam Ysabel's handling, for the big sergeant had a direct, blunt and very effective way of enforcing his demands. So Heimer, limping slightly, went to the sorrel took the reins, and started to walk it.

"How the hell did he do that?" Marsden asked a grinning Red, while Dusty spoke with Ysabel. "I know a few wrestling tricks, but that——"

"Uncle Devil's got a servant," Red explained. "Most folks reckon Tommy Okasi comes from China, but he claims to hail from some place called Nippon. Well, ole Tommy knows a mighty fancy way of fighting they use back to his home. Taught Dusty near on all he knows."

Then Marsden remembered how Dusty handled the bushwhacker, Ashley, and decided that wherever that Tommy Okasi feller came from, his way of fighting sure gave the small Texan a powerful edge over bigger and stronger men.

After a thorough walking session, Heimer returned with the sorrel and stood apprehensively by while Dusty and Marsden inspected the animal's back. While they found that the metal burr had made a small indentation where it pressed on the sorrel's back, both men realised that no permanent or serious damage had been done—which was fortunate for Heimer.

"He'll do," Dusty told the young man. "Throw the saddle on him again so that Mr. Marsden can ride him."

Although the horse fiddle-footed a little on being mounted, it soon settled down and showed signs of regaining confidence in its rider. When Marsden returned from making a circuit of the corrals, he knew he sat a horse capable of carrying him through the long and hard journey ahead.

CHAPTER SEVEN

Bushwhacker Raid

By half-past nine in the morning Elizabeth Chamberlain knew that she and her small escort were utterly and completely lost. All around them rolled the Arkansas hill country, with not a single identifiable mark. Nowhere could she see any sign of the convoy in which she travelled from Fort Downey, one of the posts established by the Union to hold the eastern half of the Indian Nations against the rebels.

A second, less palatable, thought stuck Liz—as she preferred to be called. If it came to a point, she might well blame herself for her present position. Instead of allowing the soldier at her side to concentrate on driving the buggy, she insisted on showing her views on equality by engaging him in conversation and straightening him out on various matters. While talking, they must have taken a wrong turning and, followed by three of the mounted escort, wandered away from the convoy. March discipline had not been good and the line straggled badly in the darkness, so their absence would not be discovered until dawn at the earliest.

At first Liz stubbornly refused to believe that she could

make such a mistake and when she did, both she and the escort failed to do the obvious thing—stay where they were until a search party came for them. Instead they tried to retrace their steps and in doing so became more completely and utterly lost.

"How about it, Miss Chamberlain?" asked one of the escort, a youngster in his teens. "What d'you reckon we ought to do?"

Liz thought furiously. Despite the liberal views gained by association with some of the new type of Union Army officers, she could not shake off the habits and training of a life-time. Being the daughter of the men's colonel, she felt that it rested on her shapely and beautiful head to steer them out of trouble. Her only major problem remained how she could do it.

"Could stop here and wait for a search party," the driver of the buggy suggested. "They'll be looking for us."

"No," Liz replied. "We'll make for that high ground and see if we can catch sight of our party."

None of her escort thought of questioning her decision. Obediently the driver headed the buggy up the slope at his right and the other men followed. Liz sat in silence, trying to remember something told her, or overheard, in the past.

"I suppose we're in Union-held territory," she suddenly remarked.

"The convoy had to pass pretty close to reb country," the driver replied. "That was why we moved over-night. Sure hope no reb patrol sees us."

"There's worse than reb army patrols about," one of the escort stated. "I was with a supply train that got jumped by that Captain Fog of the Texas Light. We'd stopped for water and them rebs just seemed to come up out of the ground. We didn't have a chance so the shavetail told us to throw down our guns. Them rebs never fired a shot, just took the wagons, all our horses and guns. Treated us real good. It's not their soldiers that worry me, it's them bushwhackers who're the mean ones."

Actually Dusty Fog had not been responsible for the raid in question, but his name had become so well known that every Yankee hit by the Texas Light Cavalry gave him credit for the affair.

On reaching the top of the slope, Liz's party halted and began to scan the broken, rolling bush-dotted land for some hint of where they might find their convoy. Nothing met their eye except the thinly wooded Arkansas hills, rolling slopes broken by ravines and gashes, ideal country for hiding in, but no comfort when lost on possible enemy ground.

Low-growled curses reached Liz's ears as the escort fell slightly away from the covered-over buggy and discussed their situation. She became suddenly and chillingly aware of her own position as a lone, unprotected, attractive young woman with a quartet of scared young men who had little chance of contact with the opposite sex.

A small, dainty hat perched on Liz's head. Being at the stage where defiance of conventions seems the only way of life, she wore her straw coloured hair cut short and boyishly around her truly beautiful face. The clothes selected for the journey, white frilly bosomed shirt, black jacket, tan divided skirt and dainty black riding boots, clung to a shapely body, emphasising the rich curves. All in all she must look as desirable as water in the desert to those four young man. If they once panicked and decided to desert, they might also——

Liz's thoughts died away as an uneasy feeling came over her. Once, in her sixteenth year, she had been at her father's militia camp and, believing herself to be alone, stripped naked to swim in the cool waters of a stream. While swimming, she became conscious of the felling that somebody was watching her. A search of the area revealed nothing, but later she learned that a party of soldiers had been on a nearby ridge, studying her through a telescope.

The same feeling crept over Liz again, but although she searched the area, she saw no sign of possible watchers.

Then she remembered the thought which had nagged at her on the way up the slope. More than once she had heard men talk of the importance of not appearing on a sky-line when in hostile country. Now she sat in a buggy, out in plain view on a rim.

"Nothing," said the driver. "They must have missed us buy this time."

"We'll go back into the valley," Liz answered. "Keep going until we find water, then make camp. The convoy's scout ought to be able to track us."

Once again the men obeyed her. On reaching the foot of the slope, they turned and continued their journey along the rough trail. Ahead lay the mouth to one of the ravines which split into the slope, bush-dotted, rock-covered and somehow menacing. With each stride of the horse, Liz felt her apprehension growing and the belief that somebody watched them increased.

Even as Liz opened her mouth to mention her thoughts to the driver, shots crashed from the bushes at the side of the trail. Liz saw two of the escort pitch out of their saddles. Beyond the men, bearded shapes showed among the bushes, guns roaring in hands.

"Bushwhackers!" yelled her driver and grabbed for the buggy whip.

He needed no such inducement to speed. Spooked by the sudden noise, stink of gunpowder and blood, the harness horse lunged forward and started to run, almost jerking the wheels from the ground as it hit leather. More shots came. Holes appeared in the canvas cover of the buggy, but none of the lead struck home. The last member of the escort proved less fortunate. Caught in the head and chest by bullets, the soldier slid down from his spooked horse and landed limply upon the ground.

Tearing by the mouth to the ravine, Liz saw more shapes; this time mounted on horses. Wild yells rang out and the horsemen gave chase, charging their mounts out of the ravine. One fact began to register in her mind. The attackers wore civilian clothing. No matter how poorly made it might be, the regular Confederate soldier always wore a uniform.

The riders, four in number, raced their horses after the speeding buggy and Liz knew it would be only a matter of time before they caught it. In fact their fast saddle mounts closed the gap with the harness horse rapidly. Shots were fired, but none hit the buggy.

Beforer they covered two hundred yards, Liz saw a rider coming up on either side of the buggy. The man at her side started to raise his revolver, gave her a second glance, grinned wolfishly and urged the horse on. At the other side of the buggy, a second rider came up. Desperately the young driver tried to yell that he surrendered. Coming in close, the bushwhacker fired once. Jerking under the impact of a .36 ball, the driver let whip and reins slide form his fingers, then he slumped forward in his seat.

Bringing his horse alongside the buggy animal, the bushwhacker tried to lean over and grab its reins. Failing, he gave a snarl, drew his revolver and fired down. A scream burst from the stricken harness horse. Its forelegs buckled under it and it went crashing down, sliding along the ground. Liz let out a cry of pity and fear. Desperately she grabbed at the side of the seat, clinging on with grim determination. Although it lurched wildly, the buggy remained upright. The driver's body toppled from its place, but Liz managed to stay in her seat.

Dust churned up, horses snorted as they came to sliding halts around the buggy. Liz saw men advancing with guns in their hands, heard surprised comments as they saw her clearly for the first time.

"Yeah," grinned the man who shot the horse, speaking through a fist-damaged mouth. "That's why I didn't drop her and shot the hoss."

"Never seed such obliging folks," another went on, eyeing Liz's body in a predatory manner. "Get sky-lined so's we know they're about. Then dog-my-cats if they don't come along towards us instead of going away and make us chase 'em."

"Now you just take your eyes off *her,* Tibby!" warned the first speaker. "Why for d'you reckon I shot the horse?"

Sick terror bit into Liz at the words and the way the man leered in her direction. She had no weapon, not even a Derringer or one of those new-fangled, light calibre, metal-cartridge Smith & Wesson revolvers which were becoming popular among Union officers. Even the buggy whip lay some distance away and far out of her reach.

Grinning evilly, the man started to move forward. Hooves drummed and Liz saw a couple more riders tearing along the valley bottom. Much to her surprise, she realised that one of the newcomers was a woman. Nor did that one offer to halt her horse and dismount. Instead, the girl kept her mount moving, causing the bushwhacker to jump back hurriedly. With superb skill, the girl halted her mount and glared at the men. Liz could barely believe her eyes, but the men actually appeared to be sheepish and perturbed by the girl's cold stare.

"You damned fools!" Jill Dodd hissed. "You crazy, stupid idiots!"

"They're Yankee soldiers," the fist-damaged man replied sullenly.

"And her?" Jill snapped.

"We didn't know she was with them."

Looking to where some of the bushwhackers were searching the bodies of their victims, Jill yelled a warning.

"Just take their guns and ammunition. You know what *he* told us."

Liz gave her rescuer a longer and more penetrating stare, wondering how such a girl came to be riding with a bunch of murderous bushwhackers. Glancing back along the trail Liz saw one of the men push a watch back into a soldier's pocket and another removing ammunition from the driver's pouch. With a shock, Liz realised that all her four companions wer dead.

"You murdered them!" she gasped.

"Killed," Jill corrected, slipping from her saddle. "They're Yankee soldiers and we're Confederates."

"They were only boys!" Liz went on.

"They were older than my brother when the Yankees murdered him," Jill answered. "And wearing arms and uniforms."

"If your brother was riding with this bushwhacker——" Liz began.

"He wasn't!" Jill interrupted. "All he did was——"

"Hey, Jill," called one of the bushwhackers. "Reckon we'd best be moving?"

"It'd be lost," she replied. "A party this small wouldn't be travelling alone and their friends'll be looking for them. Get the Yankees' horses and we'll move."

"How about that Yankee gal?" grinned the man.

The question set Jill something of a problem. She had not intended to make any more raids and was scouting when the noise of her men's gunfire brought her back on the run. Now she found herself with a prisoner. The obvious solution would be to leave the other girl to be found by her friends, but Jill saw that such an idea might not prove so easy. Firstly, that small party must have become separated from the main body and hopelessly lost or they would not have been heading into Confederate-held territory. So the search party might fail to find he girl. Another point Jill conceded was that one or more of her own men might slip away from the band, if she left the girl behind, and return to do what Jill had already prevented once.

"She rides with us," Jill stated. "At the first town, we'll turn her loose and she can be sent back to her own people."

"Be best, only I don't like being slowed by no buggy," the man answered.

"Can you ride, Yankee?" asked Jill.

"I can," admitted Liz, then stared defiance. "But I've no intention of doing so."

"Bring a horse for her!" called Jill.

Collecting one of the dead men's horses, a bushwhacker brought it to where the two girls stood facing each other. Liz decided to make as much difficulty as she could, delaying the bushwhacker's departure in the hope that a Union search party arrived and saved her.

"I won't mount!" she insisted.

"You'll mount!" Jill told her. "Or I'll damned soon make you!"

Fire flashed in two pairs of eyes as the girls glared at each other. They both crouched slightly, fingers crooking ready to grab at hair. Then Liz became aware of the way the male bushwhackers started to gather around. She read anticipation and sensual delight on each face as they watched the girls and waited for the next development. Suddenly a feeling of revulsion hit Liz and she knew she could not make a physical resistance to the other girl's demands, not with those men standing, waiting and watching every move. They would like nothing more than to see two girls fighting and she did not intend to degrade herself by so doing.

"All right," she said. "I'll ride. Can I take my travelling case with me?"

"Sure," answered Jill, sounding just a shade relieved at not being forced to tangle in a hair-tearing cat-fight with the Yankee girl. "You can take along a small bag, but we'll have to leave the rest of your gear here. If some of your folks're out looking for you, they'll find it."

All too well Jill realised the precarious nature of her position. During the two days since Ashley's death, she led the band by the force of her personality and because none of the men showed any qualities of leadership. One wrong move, a single mistake, a temporary set-back, would see the band break up and Jill deserted, if nothing worse. So she allowed Liz a face-saver out of gratitude for not being forced to take the showdown to a conclusion.

Going to the buggy, Liz walked to the rear and drew aside a cover to expose a small trunk and a box made to be strapped to a saddle. She took the latter, it contained toilet articles, a change of underclothing and a couple of blouses; all she would need during the next few days. If the bushwhackers kept their word, she could expect to be free in two days at the most and the Confederate soldiers would give her unrestricted passage to her own people.

"This's all I need," she told Jill.

"Heck!" Jill said, and a man joined them. "Strap this on the bay's saddle." After the man went to obey his orders. Jill turned back to the other girl. "Now listen good to me, Yankee. I stopped Guthrie abusing you just now. But if you try anything foolish, or make fuss for us, I won't be able to hold him back a second time. You think on it."

Liz thought on it, thought long and hard as she mounted the dead soldier's horse. Among other things, she wondered how a girl like Jill came to be riding with the bushwhackers and what gave her such a hatred for the Yankees. Once moving, Jill kept her horse alongside Liz's mount, but made no attempt at conversation. In a hollow they collected a string of half-a-dozen pack horses and then continued their interrupted journey.

During the ride Liz could not help noticing the cautious manner in which the bushwhackers rode. Scouts went out ahead, behind and upon both flanks and the rest of the party kept to low ground as much as possible. She wondered what made the party so nervous when traversing Confederate-held territory. After they had covered about two miles from the scene of the ambush, something else happened to give Liz more food for thought.

The flank scout on the left suddenly whirled his horse and came racing down to the main body. Riding to meet the man, Jill listened to his low-spoken message. To Liz it became clear that the other girl did not like what she heard. Turning, Jill galloped back to the halted party.

"Hold it here," she ordered. "And keep those horses quiet."

Then an idea came to Liz. The scout must have seen a

search party from the convoy; one of the considerable force from Jill's concern. If she could get up the ridge, or even create enough noise, help would be rushing towards her. For a moment she sat trying to think of the best way to achieve her ends. Perhaps a sudden thrust of heels into her horse's flanks might carry her through. Before Liz could make the move, a signal from Jill brought two men to her side and the bushwhacker girl moved her horse in front of the trio, bottling any way out.

"They're too far away," Jill commented. "And if you try screaming, the boys will quieten you."

One glance at the leering faces of the men told Liz that the quietening would prove mighty unpleasant. Any attempt at escape would bring a bullet into her at best. The party from which they hid could not arrive in time to save her. So, having no desire to throw her life away, she sat quietly until the scout, who returned to his position, gave the signal for them to move on again.

Once on the move, Guthrie kept his horse alongside Jill's mount and Liz listened uncomprehendingly to their conversation.

"Reckon it was him, still after us?" asked the man.

"Could be," Jill agreed.

"What about when he finds them Yankees back there?"

"They're soldiers and we only took horses and guns."

"And her!" Guthrie spat out, jerking a thumb towards Liz.

"We couldn't just leave her behind." Jill answered. "She might not've been found. He'll understand that."

"Reckon he'll give us a chance to explain?" asked the scared-looking man.

"Look!" Jill hissed. "You know my idea was to keep moving west, cross the Red and lay up in Texas for a spell. *You* had to hit those Yankees while I was out on scout. Now dry off and keep those horses moving. He'll not come too far after us and we'll be safe over the Red."

Sullenly Guthrie dropped back and Jill rode ahead without speaking to her prisoner. Liz began to wonder which Union Army officer caused such concern among the bushwhackers. During the War, only General George Armstrong Custer's name went out as a Union cavalry leader—and his fame rested on rash, but fortunate, chase-taking that, with plenty of luck, seemed to come off—certainly no Federal officer in Arkansas possessed a reputation likely to scare such a hardened bunch of roughnecks. She decided against asking any questions and the journey continued.

Towards sundown the party crossed the Red River and entered the State of Texas. However, once over the small ford, Jill insisted that they push on for a time. Not until four miles lay behind them and the moon rose palely in the sky did she give the order to halt and make camp. They had followed a small stream which joined the Red below the ford and their stopping place lay in open ground with the stream at the foot of a slope, forming a wide, deep pool. Having halted, Jill set her men to work. She had some caring for the leg-weary horses, others making a fire and starting to cook a meal, one more set about erecting a shelter tent.

"We'll be using that," she told Liz. "Look, I can either have you chained, or I'll take your word that you won't try to escape in the night. Which is it?"

Liz gave quick thought to the matter and replied, "I'll give you my word."

"Come and eat then," Jill accepted. "It won't be fancy, but it's filling."

With the meal over, the two girls retired to their tent. Neither undressed and they made their bed with Union Army ponchoes and blankets, using the earth for a mattress. Jill refused to talk much and Liz felt too tired to make any great conversational efforts. She saw that the other girl slept with the Tranter revolver gripped in her hand and felt instinctively that the move was not a pose to impress her.

Liz spent a restless night, but made no attempt to break her word. At dawn she found that the bushwhackers intended to make a late start, resting their horses after the hard work of the previous day. She stuck close to the tent, not caring to face the barrage of stares which greeted her every appearance. Time dragged by and towards noon heard Jill give the order to prepare to move.

"We'll be pulling out in half an hour," Jill remarked, entering the tent. "I don't know where the nearest town is, but well find it and leave you safe."

"Up there!' yelled a voice. "It's him!"

Instantly pandemonium reigned outside the tent. Men shouted curses, then the girls heard hooves drumming. Turning, Jill saw her band leaping afork their mounts and scattering in panic. In their haste, the men discarded belongings, left behind saddles, even. Jill looked downstream and saw an approaching party, recognising the man in the lead. Panic always proved infectious and the girl prepared to dash to one of the abandoned horses to make good her escape.

Even as Jill reached her decision, Liz took a hand in the game. From the noise, Liz guessed that the man the bushwhackers feared had arrived on the scene. It seemed that he came too late, for the male members of the band were making good their escape. Liz determined that the rebel girl would not get away. With that thought in mind, Liz hurled herself across the tent. Locking her arms around Jill's waist, Liz sent the other girl crashing through the tent's flap and brought her to the ground outside.

CHAPTER EIGHT

A Problem For Captain Fog

Riding the borrowed sorrel, Lieutenant Marsden sat in the centre of the line of men moving across the rolling Texas range country some two and a half miles beyond the Red River. To his right Dusty Fog sat afork a magnificent black stallion, a big, fine looking animal which turned Marsden almost green with envy. Beyond Dusty, Sam Ysabel rode a big strawberry roan stallion which looked meaner than all hell and matched the black's seventeen hands of grace and power. On Marsden's left came Billy Jack, then Kiowa, each sitting a big black horse of a kind only seen ridden by field-rank officers in the Union Army. All in all they were a superbly mounted body of men.

The reason for riding in like abreast with Marsden at the centre did not imply distrust of his motives. In line, only the leading horse had an unrestricted view of the ground it must traverse an each succeeding animal moved in air polluted by those proceeding it.

Since leaving the Texas Light Cavalry the previous day at just after dawn, Marsden had already received several lessons in the art of long distance fast travel by horse. He also knew the reason for Dusty's strict inspection of saddlery and animals—with great emphasis on the state of each horse's shoes, to the extent of having every animal reshod—and found himself admiring the young captain's attention to detail.

Dusty insisted that they wait until dawn had broken sufficiently for his party to see clearly as they saddled up the horses. After the first two hours at a fast trot guaranteed to wipe out any snuffiness the horses might feel, Dusty called the first halt. Not that the men rested during the halt. Instead they examined and made any necessary adjustments to packs and saddles while allowing their mounts to clear themselves and graze.

From then on the remainder of the day had been pure hard work. Alternating between riding at a trot and walking, leading the horses, the men covered mile after mile. Every hour brought a halt, the first and second short and giving the horses time to blow, but on the third hour long enough for the men to off-saddle and let each mount's back dry off, then the horses were grain fed and allowed to graze before being saddled and moved on. In that manner, they covered around forty miles the first day and, as long as the horses held out, ought to make at least thirty more each day by using the same methods. If so, they should reach the Brazos River's fork area in time to organise a search for Castle's wagons.

Moving on that morning, the party made good time until they approached the Red River ford selected by Dusty as best suited to their purposes. Sam Ysabel had been ahead to scout the small ford and he sat back from the edge, keeping under control when the others arrived.

"Bunch went across last night, Cap'n," he reported. "Fair-sized party. From the sign they kept going, followed that stream there west."

Kiowa rode by the others and wents to the river's edge, looking down at the tracks. Turning, he said, "Be about fifteen of 'em, some pack-hosses. One of 'em's a purty lil gal."

"Don't see no footprints," Ysabel remarked.

"Never yet saw a danged Comanche's could read sign," answered Kiowa with a faint mouth movement that passed as a broad friendly grin in his circle.

"Danged Injun varmints," Billy Jack put in, enjoying the inter-tribal rivalry expressed by the two sergeants.

"Ashley's bunch of bushwhackers?" guessed Dusty. "Looks like they didn't listen to me. Let's cross."

"And 'fore ole Kiowa here swells up and busts a gut with all this funning," Billy Jack went on to Ysabel. "We trailed Ashley's bunch for so long that even I can pick out their hosses' tracks."

"Paleface brother got heap big mouth," grunted Kiowa, "Side with Comanches too. I——"

"Move over!" Dusty ordered.

All levity left the men and they advanced as a unit ready to fight. The water came barely to the level of the stirrup irons and the river's bed offered a firm, safe footing so that the party experienced no difficulty in making their crossing. Nor were they opposed during the crossing and on the other side continued their journey. They followed the same line as the bushwhackers had the previous night.

"Smoke up ahead," Ysabel said, pointing. "Soon know if our Kiowa brother can read sign or not."

"Likely," Dusty replied. "It's on our line of march and I don't want to waste time going around. Remember the arrangements happen we get jumped by Yankees—even Kiowa can make a mistake."

Among other things before leaving the Texas Light Cavalry's camp, Dusty made arrangements for action should they be attacked. Not wishing to make a fight unless forced, he planned well and Marsden admitted that the small Texan thought of the best way to handle the situation.

The reference to a bushwhacker band left Marsden feeling puzzled. After the raid on the Kansas town of Lawrence, both Union and Confederate Governments disowned the various irregular bands and ordered a cessation of all guerilla activity. From the direction they took, Marsden concluded that Dusty meant to visit the Bushwhacker camp. Of course, if the smoke ahead proved to be no more than the bushwhackers', Dusty's party did not need to make a detour; and Marsden knew that every mile saved was of vital importance on their mission.

Topping the rim brought the camp into sight at a distance of almost half a mile. From all appearances the bushwhackers were preapring to move out. Men saddled horses, packed up their gear, but as yet had not struck the one tent erected.

Even as the party started down the slope, a bushwhacker saw them. His reaction came as something of a surprise to Dusty's party. Letting out a yell and pointing up the slope, the man dropped his bundle and raced towards the horses. Other men stared, yelled and instantly the camp took on the appearance of an overturned ants' nest. The bushwhackers dashed in all directions, discarding their property. One man tried to mount his horse, forgetting that he had not tightened the cinches. When the saddle slipped off, the man made no attempt to recover it. Instead he bounded afork the horse's bare back and set his spurs to work. Like leaves blown by the wind, the bushwhackers started their horses galloping in every direction, except towards Dusty and his men.

"What the hell?" asked Ysabel.

"Reckon they think we're still after 'em," answered Billy Jack.

"There's more to it than that," Dusty objected. "They must've——"

Two shapes erupted from the tent, chopping off Dusty's words half said. While he recognised one as the bushwhacker girl, he had never seen the other. Even at that distance Dusty could see the excellent quality of the second girl's clothing and guessed, if her actions proved anything, that she did not belong to the bushwhackers band.

"Land-sakes!" Billy Jack ejaculated, staring at the girls. "Just look at them go. They're worse'n a pair of Kilkenny cats."

Just what Liz expected Jill to do when tackled, she had not thought about. It may be that she thought her rescuers were so close that held would speedily be on hand to subdue the rebel girl. However, having laid hold on Jill, Liz found herself in a similar position to the man who caught a tiger by the tail, then found that he could not let go.

Taken by surprise, Jill went down with Liz clinging to her waist. Landing on her side, hurt and wild with a mixture of fear and fury, she acted instinctively. She drove back her upper elbow, catching Liz in the face and bringing a squeal of pain. A savage writhe brought Jill around to face her assailant. Blood from Liz's nose splashed down on to Jill's face as the rebel girl's hands drove instinctively for hair. On top, Liz screeched again as the top of her head seemed to burst into painful fire, taking her mind off the hurt of her nose. Like Jill, Liz had never been engaged in physical conflict—childhood scuffles excepted—but her own instinct for self-preservation took over. Even as Jill arched her back and rolled Liz over, the Union girl's hands found hair and she drove her head forward to try to bite.

On the ground the two girls twisted and rolled over and over, oblivious of the fleeing bushwhackers or approaching party. Hands alternated at tearing hair, grabbing and nipping flesh, swinging wild slaps and punches; legs waved, kicked, curled around each other, with Liz ignoring the way her skirt rode up to expose the white flesh over the top of her black stockings.

So wild with pain and fury did the girls become that neither realised they were rolling towards the bank of the stream. Vaguely they heard hooves coming towards them and faint shouts reached uncomprehending ears. Seeing the danger, Dusty sent his horse bounding forward. Before he reached the struggling girls, they tipped over the edge of the bank Locked in each other's arms, ignoring the bumps and jabs of the hard ground beneath them, they went rolling down the slope. Not until they plunged into the water did either girl realise what had happened. Their wails of shock died into soggy gurgles, for at that point the stream formed a large pool with sheer sides, as they plunged into the water and disappeared beneath the surface.

Shock caused the girls to separate, the sudden chill of the water winding them and causing them to forget their fury. Breaking the surface some distance from each other, soaking, winded and dazed, the girls stood for a moment. Then their eyes met and recognition began to return. Slowly Jill put the back of her hand to her lips and looked at the blood on it. Gasping for breath, Liz reached up to shove back her wet hair. Then each girl started through the waist-deep water towards the other, ready to resume hostilities.

"Well dog-my-cats!" Billy Jack gasped admiringly as he topped the slope and looked down. "Iffen they ain't coming to taw again, my name's——"

"Let's have 'em out," Dusty interrupted, and unstrapped his rope. "I'll take the bushwhacker gal, Billy Jack."

"Don't leave me no choice, Cap'n Dusty," grinned the sergeant-major, his own rope coming free.

Almost together the two ropes flew out and down, nooses dropping over the girls' heads and down below the level of their shoulders. Startled yells left feminine lips as they found their forward progress halted and arms pinned to sides while still some distance apart.

"Haul 'em in!" Dusty ordered.

Springing from their horses, Marsden, Ysabel and Kiowa ran to the ropes. After securing his rope to the saddlehorn, Billy Jack dropped to the ground and went to assist Marsden hauling Liz out of the water and up the slope.

"Now this here's what I call real fishing," grinned Billy

Jack, watching the two squealing girls hauled up the slope towards him.

"I wouldn't want to put either of them in a glass case on a wall though," Marsden answered.

Before they reached the top of the slope, surprise, exhaustion and realisation of pain forgotten during the wild, thrashing mêlée, drove all thoughts of further aggression from the girls. Seeing the men above her, Jill became aware of her position and wondered what her fate would be at the hands of the grim-faced young captain who killed Ashley. Dusty Fog must have been hunting for her band and would have found the bodies of the ambushed Union soldiers. If so, he knew that the bushwhackers went against his orders and continued their operations.

With the fight over, reaction bit sharply into Liz, more so than affected her opponent. Sobbing, she sank to her knees and on the rope being taken from her shoulders, covered her face with her hands. Pain nagged at her; bruises gained during the roll down the slope throbbed dully; where teeth, feet or hands connected on flesh each sent a separate sting through her and her hair roots seemed to be on fire. In that condition, she could not think and so missed the surprising detail of seeing a Union lieutenant in company with the Confederate soldiers.

"Tend to them, Kiowa," Dusty ordered. "Rest of you see to the horses. We'll make this our noon halt."

Kiowa had learned Indian-style medicine from his mother and gained something of a reputation as a curer of minor ailments. Stepping forward, he opened his saddlebag and took out his medicine kit, then went towards the girls. One glance told him that neither had sustained serious injury during the fight and also that Liz needed his services far more than did Jill.

"Just let me take a look at you, ma'am," he said gently.

At another time Liz might have objected to submitting to treatment by a man like Kiowa. In her present condition, she wanted help and willingly accepted its offer on receipt.

With surprising gentleness, Kiowa drew the girl's hands from her face and bent forward to look at the blood-trickling nose.

Forcing herself to her feet, Jill walked slowly to where Dusty stripped the saddle from his big black stallion.

"I don't see why you're hunting us down like this," she stated, holding her torn shirt together as best she could. "They were Yankee soldiers, and the boys only took their guns and horses."

"You've lost me, ma'am," Dusty answered, swinging the saddle clear. "Who were Yankee soldiers?"

"The bunch Guthrie ambushed back in Arkansas. We saw your troop while we were pulling out and heading for Texas after the ambush."

"Not my troop, ma'am," Dusty corrected, although he now saw the reason for the bushwhackers' flight on seeing him. "Who's the girl?"

"She was with the Yankees. I didn't know what Guthrie aimed to do, I was out on scout when they saw the Yankees and made their hit. Then I couldn't leave the girl alone. Brought her along and was going to leave her in the first town we found."

"How is she, Kiowa?" called Dusty.

"Mite shook up, but nothing broke or hurt too bad."

"I didn't start the fight," Jill put in. "And I wouldn't've let anything happen to her."

"I believe you," Dusty replied. "Only you should have taken my advice and left that bunch. They're not fighting the Yankees."

"They would have been," Jill insisted. "I aimed to reform the band in Texas, get men in it who wanted to fight."

"That's what the army's for," Dusty said. "Have you any dry clothes?"

"Sure."

"Go change into them. See if you can get your prisoner into something dry."

"What do you intend to do with me?" asked Jill.

"Lady," admitted Dusty. "That's something I haven't figured out yet. Go get dried off and changed."

Turning, Jill walked away. She went to where Liz sat on the ground and looked down. Almost with relief Jill saw that the Yankee girl seemed to be recovering and in no danger. A little stiffly, she ordered to fit Liz out with dry clothing. While Liz first thought of refusing, she realised —through her exploring fingers—that her blouse had suffered damage in the fight and that she needed to get out of the wet clothing. So, just as stiffly as Jill offered, Liz accepted.

Thought had returned to Liz with Kiowa's ministrations and she looked about her, seeing much that was puzzling. The bushwhackers had all fled, but from Confederate, not Union soldiers; and a small party at that. Then Liz became aware of Marsden and wondered at his presence. At first she thought he might be a prisoner, yet knew of no prisoner-of-war camp in Texas. Also no prisoner would be under the escort of a captain and three senior non-coms.

Still pondering on Marsden's presence, Liz followed Jill into the tent. While accepting the other's offer to dry clothing, Liz maintained frigid silence and Jill did nothing to help. Opening her war bag, Jill produced two shirts and a couple of pairs of men's pants, remarking that she had nothing else to offer. Liz opened her travelling case and took out dry underwear and a towel.

While stripping off her clothes, Liz could hear enough to tell her that the men were tending to their horses. As she started to dry herself with the towel, she caught the sound of voices; one a southern drawl, the other a northern accent. Apparently the two officers were in conference and she strained her ears to catch what they discussed.

"So the bushwhacker girl brought the other one with her." The small man with the southern drawl was speaking. "Showed good sense in doing it too. The other girl might never've been found—or one of the bushwhackers gone back to her."

"You believe the girl intended to release Miss Chamberlain?" asked Marsden, having recognised Liz as an acquaintance from Little Rock's army social circle.

"Sure. That girls' no bushwhacker slut," Dusty replied. "And she'd a hold on that rabble or Miss Chamberlain'd've been raped before now."

"Thing now is what do you aim to do with them?"

"How's that, mister?"

"We can't leave them here," Marsden pointed out, then went on. "Could find a town, like the girl intended."

"There's none around and we're too far north for the main Texas-Arkansas trails," Dusty answered.

"If the girl can control her men, leave them both here," Marsden suggested.

"And if the men don't come back?"

"Reckon they won't, sir?"

"Nope. They'll figure that I've taken the girls with me and destroyed the camp. So the girls will have to come with us."

"Can they stand up to the pace?"

"Mister," Dusty said quietly but grimly, "they'll have to stand up to it. You know as well as I do what's at stake."

"Yes, sir," agreed Marsden. "Couldn't we leave them at either Dallas or Fort Worth?"

"It'd take us a day out of our way. We don't have a day to spare, mister."

"Then let one of the men——"

"I'd thought of it. But there's nobody I can spare. Even without being short-handed if it comes to a fight, and needing them to deal with the Indians. Sam Ysabel's our best man with the pack animals and Kiowa's got the medicine skill of we need it. And Billy Jack can cold-shoe a horse as well as many a blacksmith. It just won't do, mister."

"How about me?" asked Marsden.

"You're no plainsman, mister,"Dusty answered. "And you'd not get far travelling through Texas in *that* color uniform. No, mister, those girls will have to take their choice. Stay here and chance being found—or come with us and stick the pace. There's no other way and to much at stake for me to do otherwise."

Watching Dusty, Marsden felt sympathy with the other's position and knew just what moral fibre it needed to make such a decision. Reared in the strict Southern tradition, Dusty did not lightly toss aside his training on the subject of women's treatment. However, the small Texan had to balance two lives against the chances of preventing an Indian uprising which would bring death, or worse, to thousands of men, women and children.

"Go pick the best two horses from the bushwhacker remuda." Dusty ordered. "I want the rest of their stock scattered and all this stuff destroyed if the girls agree to come along with us. See to it, mister."

In the tent Liz looked at Jill who donned a pair of men's long-legged red flannel underwear.

"Who is that small captain?" she asked.

While he might have broken up her bushwhacker band, Jill still felt considerable pride in the small Texan's reputation as a Confederate soldier.

"Captain Dusty Fog," she answered a shade pompously.

Liz tossed aside her towel and started to dress. Thoughts churned in her head as she slipped on the dry underclothing. She knew Dusty Fog's reputation and felt certain that something very important lay behind the captain's presence so far from the battlefields of Arkansas. The scrap of conversation she heard confirmed her belief and she felt cold anger well inside her as she realised that the Union officer must be a traitor. He seemed to know her, which meant they must have met. Swiftly Liz finished dressing, feeling uncomfortable in men's clothing. She stepped to the door of the tent and raised the flap a trifle.

"Jackson Marsden!" she breathed.

While visiting in Little Rock, Liz had met Marsden and heard him mentioned as a promising career officer. Only something of great importance would turn such a man into a traitor. From what she overheard, the mission the men rode on was of vital significance with time its essence for success.

Ever since the death of the soldiers, Liz had felt guilty, blaming herself for them getting lost in the first place. Now she saw a chance to partially make amends. She would go with the Texans and do everything in her power to make sure that their mission did not succeed.

"I'd like to see you ladies outside when you're dressed," Dusty called, standing outside the tent.

A smile played on Liz's lips. Captain Fog thought his problem with herself and the other girl was over—she aimed to see that it had only just begun.

CHAPTER NINE

A Clash Of Wills

"You must understand, ladies," Dusty told the girls. "I refuse to allow considerations of your sex to slow me down. If you come with us, it is on the understanding that you obey my orders and accept my conditions. We'll be covering between thirty and forty miles a day and that's rough on a *man*."

Looking around her, Jill gave a shrug. Although Dusty had not mentioned the nature of his mission, she knew it must be very important for him to lay down such terms to a pair of girls. She decided that she could make a sacrifice for the Confederate States.

"I accept your conditions, Captain Fog," she said.

"Do you, Miss Chamberlain?" asked Dusty.

"Yes," Liz replied.

Something in the girl's voice drew Marsden's eyes to her and he felt puzzled by her mild acceptance. Although he did not know her too well, Marsden figured Liz to be an intelligent young woman. In which case she must know of the importance of the Texans' misson—although not the details of it. He knew her to be almost fanatically loyal to the Union, due in some measure to the kind of friends she made among the intellectual Southerner-hating set of volunteer officers. So Liz should be protesting, demanding immediate return to her own people and relying on Southern chivalry to get her way; or at least trying to delay the party's departure by argument. The manner in which she surrendered to the inevitable worried Marsden.

Taking advantage of the delay, Billy Jack and Sam Ysabel had cooked a meal from the bushwhackers' supplies and the party ate well. After the meal, Dusty set his men to work. Jill helped saddle the horses while the men fitted the pack saddles on the baggage animals, but Liz stayed out of the way. Instinctively Liz knew the moment for defiance had not yet arrived and so remained meekly obedient.

Before moving out, Dusty saw that all the bushwhackers' property was destroyed and their remuda scattered. He did not intend to leave them the means to reorganize should they return to their camp-site.

"From now on you tend to your own mount, Miss Chamberlain," he said.

"Of course, Captain," she replied.

"Mount up, then. You'll ride at my right, Miss Chamberlain, you at the left, Miss Dodd."

Jill swung astride her spirited buckskin gelding and Liz mounted the kettle-bellied bay mare assigned to her, feeling just a trifle self-conscious and aware that she filled out her borrowed pants rather well. However, none of the men appeared to be interested in how she looked and she concentrated on handling her horse.

On moving out from the destroyed camp, Liz found herself with Dusty at one side and Marsden upon the other. She realised that she ought to be showing some interest in his presence.

"May I ask how you come to be here, Mr. Marsden?" she asked. "Are you a prisoner?"

"No, Miss Chamberlain," Marsden replied.

"Then what are you, a traitor?"

"You might say that," Marsden agreed.

A low hiss left the girl's lips and anger glowed in her eyes. "Do you think betraying your country and your honour is worth the monetary gains you receive?"

"I'm not doing it for money," Marsden replied.

"Then why do you, a supposedly loyal Union officer, betray your own country?"

"Because——"

"He has a good reason, Miss Chamberlain," Dusty put in. There was no point in letting the girls know the true nature of the assignment. Even now there might be a chance of a south-bound party to take the girls off his hands, in which case they probably would talk and he did not wish to start panic among the people of Texas.

"I'd like to hear it," Liz snapped.

"Maybe you will, one day," answered Dusty.

Sensing that further questions would be ignored, Liz let the matter drop and concentrated upon handling her horse. Holding to a steady trot, the party covered three miles before Liz saw a chance to put her delaying tactics into operation.

"Dismount and walk," Dusty ordered.

Every eye turned to Liz as she remained in her saddle when all but she and Dusty swung to the ground.

"I won't!" she stated. "I refuse to walk!"

She took a gamble on her knowledge of southern chivalry. With the camp back on the stream destroyed, and no sight of human habitation from one horizon to the other, the men would not leave her behind. So she aimed to delay them by argument, stir up trouble among them. If Dusty Fog allowed her to ride, it would make discontent among the others. Also riding would tire her horse—to be fair, she took no pleasure in the thought of inflicting suffering upon her mount—and she knew the speed of the party could be no faster than the pace of the slowest member.

So Liz prepared for a clash of will with Dusty Fog, looked forward to testing him and learning just how far she might go.

Edging his horse towards Liz's mount, Dusty suddenly reached out and gripped her by the waist. Like many people when first coming into contact with Dusty, Liz failed to appreciate the powerful nature of his frame. Taken by surprise both at Dusty's prompt action and his strength, Liz felt herself lifted, swung from the saddle and lowered to the ground.

"I still won't walk!" she shouted and flung herself into a sitting position on the ground.

Dusty did not even give the girl a glance. "Sergeant-major!" he snapped. "Take Miss Chamberlain's horse."

"Yo!" Billy Jack replied.

"I refuse to walk!" Liz warned, conscious that every eye was on her.

"Give me the word and I'll drag her along by the hair, Captain," Jill said.

"Move out!" Dusty ordered, ignoring the girl's suggestion.

Only Jill failed to obey the order immediately. As the men stepped off, she stood for a moment, throwing glanced first at Dusty, then towards Liz. Although town-raised, Jill had heard often enough of the dangers of being left afoot on the open plains of Texas. Since leaving the camp, the party came across several large bunches of half-wild longhorned Texas cattle and Dusty warned that such animals feared only a mounted human being; and the cattle were but one of the dangers to a girl afoot.

"Don't be a fool, Yankee," she urged. "Captain Fog's not bluffing."

"And neither am I," Liz replied grimly.

Giving an angry snort, Jill started to turn. Then she gave a shrug, drew the Tranter—picked up by Billy Jack at the camp—and ordered it butt forward to Liz.

"Here, you're more likely to need it than I am."

For once in her life Liz felt at a loss for words. Taking the Tranter, Liz watched Jill turn and walk away leading the buckskin. Setting her teeth grimly, Liz prepared to call Dusty Fog's bluff.

"You can't just walk away and leave her," Jill said, catching up with Dusty.

"It's her choice," he replied.

Like Liz, Dusty knew the clash of their wills had begun. While he could appreciate her motives and admire her guts, he refused to be swayed from his purpose. If he showed weakness, Liz would come to expect it. For the sake of his mission, he must break the girl's defiance and aimed to do it.

Nursing the Tranter as she sat on the ground, Liz watched the party walking away from her. Not one of them gave a sign of being aware of her absence and she set her face in an expression of determination. Slowly she looked around and a feeling of awe crept over her as she studied the vast, open, rolling miles of land around her. Apart from the party walking away, she could see no sign of human life, not so much as a far-distant smudge of smoke hinting at a house's presence.

A momentary fear crept into her as she realised how precarious her position would be if the small Texan refused to back down. For hundreds of miles all she could expect would be deadly danger. The buffalo wolf, the black bear, even the mountain lion under certain conditions, could be dangerous to a lone traveller. Nor would many of the human beings she might meet prove any more of a blessing. She had escaped rape at the hands of the bushwhackers once, but what if they found her alone and without Jill Dodd's protection? True Liz held a gun, but she knew just how little defence it would give in her unskilled hands.

"Take hold of yourself, girl," she told herself. "He'll break and come back for you."

"Keep moving, Miss Dodd," Dusty growled as Jill

slowed her pace and started to turn her head. "Don't look back!"

Jerking herself around, Jill turned a worried, pleading face towards the small Texan. "You can't just desert her, Captain."

"And I can't waste time on her little games either," Dusty replied.

"Is what you're doing so important that it's worth the life of an innocent girl?" Jill demanded hotly.

"Take my word, Miss Dodd," Marsden put in. "It is important."

"How would you know?" Jill snapped, her smouldering hate of Union supporters driving her on.

"Because Mr. Marsden gave up his career, and that's as important as his life to him, to bring us news that started this mission," Dusty growled.

"Then you *are* one of our spies," the girl gasped.

"No, ma'am!" Marsden replied.

"Then why——" Jill began, stopping speaking when she realised that she could not make herself continue with the question or why he turned traitor.

"Because Mr. Marsden learned something real important, Miss Dodd," Dusty explained, and Jill writhed at the scorn and fury in his voice. "Something that, unless stopped, will cost thousands of innocent men, women and children their lives. That's why he turned 'traitor' and came to us."

Contrition bit into the girl and she looked at Marsden. "I'm sorry. More sorry than I can tell you."

"Forget it, Miss Dodd," answered Marsden. "And remember that Captain Fog is doing what he must."

"Couldn't you have told the Yank—Miss Chamberlain about your mission, Captain?" asked Jill. "Surely if she knew how important——"

"She might not try to delay us," Dusty admitted. "But I can't risk taking time to explain and then have her cause me more trouble to delay me."

"Would she still try if she knew?" Jill said.

"Put yourself in her place," Dusty answered. "Suppose you learned something that put you in a position to help the South to victory. Would you try to do i?"

"Of course."

Even after so short a time Dusty had come to know enough about Jill to make an argument she would understand. He wanted to stop her talking about Liz and reckoned that such an argument might bring off the desired result.

"So would Miss Chamberlain," he said, cementing the idea in Jill's head. "And that's why I won't let her delay us."

Suddenly Jill realised what a strain Dusty must be under at having to make such a decision. Being born and raised in Texas, he knew even better than Jill the dangers to a person left afoot on the range. Jill set her teeth, fixed her eyes on the forward horizon and fought down her desire to look back. Flickering glances at the men on either side of her she read their concern from the tight-set faces. Only the knowledge of their mission and the respect they felt for their leader kept them walking on, leaving Liz behind, as Dusty ordered.

With growing disbelief and anxiety Liz watched the party continue to walk away. A quarter of a mile separated them and grew on to the half-mile mark. Every step they took, Liz expected to see them halt, look back, possibly one of them return to plead with her for a change of mind. Yet each step saw them going further from her, increasing the distance with relentless precision.

A movement to her right caught the corner of her eye. Swinging around, she saw a small band of pronghorn antelope stepping daintily through the bush-dotted range about two hundred yards away. Even as she looked, something startled the animals and they broke in a wild, scattering, leaping flight. Liz felt a momentary panic, wondering what spooked the antelope and knowing she could not equal their speed should the unseen menace come her way.

"He'll turn back soon," she told herself, but with less conviction than on the last occasion she used the sentiment.

At that moment her eyes caught another movement. Turning, she gave a low cry of horror and stared at a diamondback rattlesnake all of three foot long as it glided through the buffalo grass some yards from her. Liz came hurriedly to her feet. The vibrations of her rising halted the snake, bringing it into a defensive coil while the interconnecting horny caps which formed its rattle giving out their vicious buzz-saw warning. Choking down a little sob, Liz started to walk as fast as she could after the departing party.

"That's a might stubborn lil gal, Sam," Billy Jack remarked after they had covered something over half a mile since leaving Liz.

"Sure," agreed Ysabel. "Only this time she's met somebody a damned sight more stubborn."

If Dusty heard the men, he ignored them. Mouth set in grim, determined lines, he fought down his inclination to turn back. However, one of the party had not been under Dusty's kind of discipline long enough to stick rigidly to obedience of orders. Having fought down the inclination as long as she could, Jill chanced a quick glance to the rear.

"She's coming after us!" Jill said, letting out a gasp of relief and showing neither jubilation nor derision at Liz's defeat.

"Keep your eyes to the front and stay marching," Dusty growled.

Catching the faint note of relief in Dusty's voice, Jill felt no resentment at his brusque tone. Was it her imagination, or did Dusty slow his pace? She could not be sure. With a woman's instincts, she saw beneath the stony exterior and grim determination, reading Dusty's feelings at the course of action forced on him. Whatever business took him west, it must be mighty important to make him treat a girl as he had Liz. A shudder ran through her as she remembered what Dusty said about the thing he must stop costing thousands of innocent lives. While she could not imagine what it might be, she felt the growing urgency with which Dusty pressed on to the west and knew he meant what he said.

Behind the party Liz increased her pace to a fast walk. Her cheeks reddened a little as she wondered what kind of reception the others would give her. Probably they would mock her. The little rebel slut was going to——The weight of the Tranter stopped that line of thought and Liz remembered just how much she owed to Jill Dodd.

Going down a slope which took them out of Liz's sight, Dusty looked at his party. "Halt!" he called. "We'll rest up here for a spell."

"I need it," Jill groaned.

"The hosses get the rest, ma'am," grinned Kiowa. "We work."

"Billy Jack, tend to Miss Chamberlain's horse this time," Dusty ordered.

"Yo!" the sergeant-major replied. "Get your hoss's nose-bag out of the saddle pouch, Miss Dodd. Sam'll give you the grain."

Clearly the men knew their duties, for none needed telling what to do. Each of them took his horse's nose-bag from the saddle pouches and Sam Ysabel led the way to one of the pack animals. Carefully he opened one of the grain sacks on the right of the pack saddle and started to pour a quantity of food into each bag as it was offered to him.

"Round the other side, ma'am," he said as Jill came up in her turn.

For a moment the order puzzled Jill, then she realised that the load must be balanced if the horse's back was to be kept free from injury. Jill did not know it, but a difference of as little as two pounds in the weight of the packs could injure the horse. However, of necessity, Sam Ysabel had learned the pack train trade very thoroughly and could gauge a balance with his eyes as well as many men would do with a set of scales.

Taking the feed-bag to the buckskin, Jill happened to glance inside as she prepared to place it into position. She saw something brown among the grain and reached in to extract a small ball of what appeared to be wood.

"What're you doing, gal?" asked Billy Jack as she prepared to toss the object away.

"I found it mixed in with the grain," she explained.

"Sure. We put it there. It's meat."

Meat?" Jill gasped. "But horses don't eat meat."

"Don't set down and carve a pot-roast, ma'am," agreed Ysabel. "But the Comanches learned way back that slipping some small balls of meat in with the other food helps a hoss to keep going when it's travelling fast."

"Get those nose-bags on there," Dusty called. "Buckle it up good and tight, Miss Dodd, so he doesn't have to toss his head to get at the grain and lose most of it."

Removing her horse's bit, Jill fixed the nose-bag in position and drew it up tight. The horses had been allowed to drink when crossing a small stream some three hundred yards back and the buckskin started eating as she drew on the bag. After caring for her own mount, Jill looked around to see if she could help with any of the others. Finding that the men had cared for all the stock, she gave thought to her own needs.

"I've got to go into the bushes," she remarked and Dusty nodded.

"Let me take your horse, Miss Dodd," Marsden offered.

Jill's fingers brushed against Marsden's as she handed over the reins. A tingling sensation ran through her and she lifted her eyes to his. Then she remembered that the Yankees had murdered her brother and tried to fight the feeling down. Turning, she walked hurriedly up the slope and into a clump of bushes near the top. Since joining the bush-whackers, most of her toilet arrangements were made in a similar manner. Then she always kept her Tranter handy and felt uneasy at the thought that the gun was in Liz's hands. However, she guessed that the Texans would respect her privacy and went out of sight to attend to her business.

With set face and grim bearing, Liz walked down the slope towards the men. Jill came from the bushes adjusting her waist belt and Liz braced herself for the first of the expected taunts.

"I'll take the Tranter, Yankee," Jill remarked in a neutral tone. "And if you want to go, I'd go now, Captain Dusty'll be wanting to move off real soon."

Handing Jill the gun, Liz disappeared into the bushes and soon the two girls walked side by side down the slope. Although Liz's back remained stiff with defiance, she found none of the expected derision. A feeling of pique hit her, a touch of disappointment, as she found that she could not even feel like a martyr suffering at the hands of a vicious enemy.

Looking around, Dusty saw that his force had everything ready to move and so gave the order to march. Liz swung into her saddle and wondered at the sense of security the touch of leather and presence of the rest of the party gave her. Quick thought warned her not to try any more delaying tactics right then. When they made camp for the night might offer greater opportunities. However, her annoyance at being ignored—when she had worked herself up to take derision if not actual abuse—drove her to pick on somebody. Marsden, in his Union blue uniform, provided her with the best target.

"Mr. Marsden," she said. "Didn't you command the rearguard action at Poison Springs?"

"Yes, ma'am."

"You handled it magnificently, so I heard. There were

many rebel casualties," she went on in a carrying voice, then turned to look at Kiowa. "Were you at the action, Sergeant?"

"No, ma'am," Kiowa answered.

"Were any of the Texas Light Cavalry?"

"Three companies."

"Did you see any of them, Mr. Marsden?" Liz asked.

"If you mean, did he help kill any of our outfit," Dusty put in coldly. "I'd say it was likely. A soldier's duty is to kill his enemies. Only we're not fussing with him for what happened in the past."

A flush crept over Liz's face as she realised that she had instinctively made a move to split up the party, and saw it fail. Once more her anger turned on Marsden. "I fail to see why a man like you turned traitor and renegade!" she snapped.

"You leave him be, Yankee!" Jill shouted across Dusty. "He must've had a real good reason."

"He had, ma'am," agreed Billy jack. "If Castle gets them Injuns——"

"Billy Jack!" Dusty roared, but knew that the damage had been done. "That's why we're heading west in such a hurry, ma'am. Two of your officers are trying to stir up an Injun uprising in Texas."

"Carney Castle's scheme!" Liz gasped. "I heard him mention it. Why it would bring about the withdrawal of all the Texas troops from the rebel army. You lousy traitor, Marsden. You told the rebs—"

"Keep in line, Dodd!" Dusty barked as Jill started to swing her horse with the intention of resuming hostilities. Turning back to Liz he continued, "Mr. Marsden knows what such an uprising would mean. Understands the cost in innocent lives. The men behind the idea don't, or they'd never have started it."

"You rebels have used Indians to do your fighting for you," she pointed out.

"Pike's Cherokee Brigade," agreed Dusty. "That's not the same thing——"

"Why?" spat Liz. "Because they sided you rebs——"

"No, ma'am. Because the Cherokee aren't Comanche, Kiowa or Kaddo."

"They scalped our dead on the field of Pea Ridge," Liz reminded him.

"They did, ma'am," Dusty answered. "Which's just what I mean. The Cherokee are tamed Indians. They've lived white-man fashion for years. Most of 'em are Christians, send their kids to school. Yet when they went to war, they went right back to the old ways and started scalping."

"Cap'n Dusty's right, ma'am," Ysabel put in. "them Cherokee're tamed Injuns and like lap-dogs alongside buffalo-wolves when took with Comanches, Kiowas and Kaddos like the fool Yankees're trying to stir up. At least our Cherokees stuck to killing and lifting hair from Yankee *soldiers*."

"Those hostiles Castle plans to stir up, ma'am," Dusty said quietly. "Once they get started, they'll not leave a living white in Texas."

"And a thing like that won't just stay in Texas. Word'll go out and every hostile across the country'll paint for war," Ysable warned grimly. "They'll likely not be a white man, woman or child left alive from the Red River to the Pacific. That's why we're headed west."

Liz relapsed into silence and thought of what the men told her. Although she knew little about Castle's scheme, she had met the man. Thinking back, she remembered hearing him discuss the effects of an Indian uprising in Texas. The withdrawal of the Texas troops could bring victory for the Union. Castle made it clear that such an uprising would need to be controlled, the Indians held in check and directed only at profitable targets. Of course, the rebels would try to stop such a plan, nor would they hesitate to try to blacken the Union's name by pretending the situation was far more serious and endangered the life of their people. Naturally the Texans would try to make her believe in the danger. She refused to be swayed from her purpose and determined to help the Union cause by doing all she could to prevent Dusty Fog's party interfering with Castle's war-winning scheme.

No chance presented itself during the rest of the day's march. Liz walked slowly to the camp-fire after tending to her horse at the end of the day. As she sat down, a thought struck her. She would stay awake and when all the others slept release and scatter the horses.

CHAPER TEN

You're Playing A Game, Miss Chamberlain—Don't

"Come on, Yankee," said a voice, while a hand shook Liz's shoulder and jarred through her sleep. "Time to be up and doing."

Cold grey light met Liz's eyes as they came open. Stifling a low groan, for the ground proved a far less satisfactory matress than her bed at home offered, she forced herself up on one elbow and peered around sleepily. The men gathered around a fire and held plates, while a coffee pot bubbled on the flames.

"You sure slept well last night," Jill went on, with a friendly smile. "Why even afore we set camp, you'd gone off. Didn't disturb you, not that we could have."

"So much for my big idea!" thought Liz, tossing aside the blankets and rising stiffly. It seemed that she slept through the night instead of laying awake until a chance presented itself for her to free and scatter the horses.

"Here. I'll lend you a hand to pack your bedroll," Jill offered. "You can't eat until it's done."

"Thanks, reb," Liz answered, suddenly feeling ravenously hungry and sniffing at the aroma of cooking meat that wafted from the fire.

With the bedroll packed ready for loading, Liz walked with Jill towards the fire. It came as something of a surprise to see a smile on Dusty Fog's face.

"Good morning, Miss Chamberlain," he greeted. "How do you feel?"

"I'd like a hot bath and a buggy to ride in," she found herself replying, "but apart from that I'm fine."

"You can have the hot bath, happen we find some warm-water springs," Dusty told her with a grin. "But buggies're something we're long out of."

"So much for Southern hospitality," she sighed, but her voice held no anger or bitterness.

"Comes the end of the War, ma'am," Dusty answered, "happen you're in the Rio Hondo country, I'll fix you with a buggy that's soft and comfortable as swan's down, rig you a bath too, but you'll have to take it by yourself."

"I should hope so, for shame," she chuckled.

Suddenly she thought how incongruous the situation had become, for her to be standing exchanging pleasantries with a man who only yesterday deserted her and whose vitally important mission she intended to ruin if she could.

"Sure hope these pronghorn steaks are all right, ma'am," Billy Jack said, handing her a plate. "I'd rather have it hung for a couple of days, but Cap'n Dusty allows there's not time for that. Eggs aren't too bad though."

"Pronghorn? Eggs" she breathed. "But where——'

"Sam got one last night," Billy Jack explained. "Pronghorn I mean."

During the meal, an idea began to form in Liz's mind for making trouble among the party. However, before she could make a move towards starting, Dusty saw that she had finished eating and gave orders to prepare for moving.

"Can you manage, ma'am?" asked Ysabel as she walked towards her saddle.

Seeing Kiowa hovering in the background, Liz shook her head. "I—I'm not sure if I can."

"Sergeant Ysabel!" Dusty barked. "Tend to your duties. Kiowa, help him. Mr. Marsden, help the ladies—only don't pamper them."

"Yo!" Marsden replied.

"Go help the Yankee, Mr. Marsden," Jill suggested as he came in her direction. *"I'm* not so milk-soft that I can't saddle and tend for my own horse."

In her desire to stifle a growing tolerance and liking felt towards at least one Yankee, Jill said the right thing. Annoyance glinted in Liz's eyes and she forgot her pose of the meek, near-helpless female in the presence of strong, reliable men. Taking up her saddle and bedroll, she stamped indignantly towards the mare. Determination to show the rebel that anything a Southern girl could do, a Yankee could do better, drove her to forget her plan and also the aches in her saddle-stiffened body.

On reaching the horses, she found that releasing them in the night would not have been such an easy task. The Union Army always picketed their horses, the Texans preferred to give their mounts a certain amount of freedom to move and graze. All the men's mounts had chain hobbles on their forelegs, a leather cuff buckled around each leg over the pastern joint and connected by a short swivel chain which let the animal move around at a slow walk in order to pick good grazing. To remove the hobbles in the dark would take much time and could only be done with some noise.

Liz found the bay and Jill's buckskin secured in a different manner, though not one easier to remove than the chain hobbles would be. A loop of rope encircled the mare's neck secured with a bowline knot that rested on the left shoulder. From there the rope went down to be taken in a half-hitch around the ankle joint of the left hind leg and carried back up to join and knot about the neck looped in a manner which raised the hoof about four inches above the ground.

"Didn't have any spare gear along, ma'am," Billy Jack apologised as she glared pointedly at his horse's fore feet. "Had to use a scotch hobble on your ladies' mounts. Watch that half hitch on the legs. It stops the horse kicking free, but it's surely hell to get off."

After freeing the mare's leg, Liz prepared to saddle up. While taking up her saddle blanket, she saw another chance to delay the party; although not one she cared to use. However, she must put loyalty to her country before her dislike at inflicting deliberate suffering upon her horse. She knew the purpose of the blanket, to give protection and padding to the horse's back against the weight and pressure of the saddle. To do this correctly, the blanket must be raised slightly off the back-bone and withers and also, very important, laid flat on the back without wrinkles. Taking up the blanket, she made sure that the underside held a ridge of raised material which would chafe and rub into the mare's body, making her back sore.

Just as Liz put the blanket on, she felt a violent shove and heard Jill's contempt-filled voice at her side.

"Land-sakes, Yankee, don't you know a damned thing? Her, let me put your saddle on for you."

Hot anger flared up in Liz, reddened her cheeks and brought her fingers into a hair-grabbing crook. Before she could move, a hand caught her arm and she turned to glare fury up into Marsden's face.

"Drop it, Miss Chamberlain," he warned.

"I don't know what——" Liz began.

"Stop this playing at being the saviour of the Union."

"*Playing!* she gasped.

"Playing!" repeated Marsden coldly. "You're playing a game, Miss Chamberlain—Don't. Captain Fog won't let you delay him. If he'd seen what you just did, he'd maybe have given you what you deserve."

Despite herself, Liz felt a shudder run through her, for

she knew the punishment meted out to a soldier who negligently or deliberately allowed his horse to get a sore back. He was stripped naked and strapped into the saddle, then made to ride that way until he knew how the horse felt. Glancing to where Dusty saddled his black stallion, Liz wondered if he would treat her in such a manner and decided he might. She wondered if perhaps he might have been telling the truth about the ultimate result of Castle's plan. Then she gave an angry shake of her head. No, Dusty Fog only made up the story of a wholesale Indian slaughter of innocents as a way of playing on her emotions and gaining her co-operation. A man with Castle's sense of social conscience and belief in the rights of the individual would never chance any scheme that might endanger innocent lives.

Snarling that she could handle the mare without further help, Liz thrust by Jill and continued the saddling.

Once again the party continued with its westwards march and the girls learned just how rough such a trip could be. Alternately riding with walking, the halts spent checking hooves, condition, saddlery or feeding and watering the horses, Dusty led his party and covered over thirty miles each day. With each passing mile, his hope of meeting a south-bound party to whom he might deliver the girls grew less and less. Since the War took so many men from Texas, people tended to concentrate in or around the towns and cities and did little travelling. So, although he hated having to subject the girls to such continuous effort, he continued to hold his pace.

And it was an effort for both girls, although Liz felt the effects more than did Jill. While healthy and used to an open-air life, Liz found a vast difference between taking a long ride in the morning and making thirty miles a day with the care of her horse awaiting her attention at the end of the trip. Under those conditions she found little time for plotting further delaying tactics. In fact, during her scant leisure hours she felt no inclination to waste time in planning ideas that would need further bodily effort to carry out. Her life became a continuous struggle against weariness and pain as unused muscles protested and stiffened under the strain. When in camp, she finished her work, ate her food and dropped into her blankets to sleep like a log. Only Liz's determination not to let the rebel girl see her give way kept her moving when her body screamed to be let collapse on the ground and move no more.

Due to her life with the bushwhackers, Jill felt the strain somewhat less than did Liz; not that Jill found keeping up the pace easy and often had to use Liz's presence as an inducement to keep going.

The men did what they could to ease the girls' burden, but all had more than enough work on their hands and both Jill and Liz were compelled to attend to much of the care and attention their horses needed.

Three days went by, long, hard days, and with each Marsden found his admiration for the Texans' skill as horsemasters growing. He watched everything and learned much that would be of use to him in his career as a soldier. From the range-wise men he learned which plants and roots possessed medicinal value, what certain animal signs meant in the way of finding food and water on the open plains. Everybody in the Union Army knew that the end of the Civil War would mark the beginning of westward movement on to the Great Plains home of several hostile Indian tribes. With the knowledge he gained on the trip, Marsden knew he could be of the greatest use in the future campaigns. Such a thought always brought on a fit of brooding as he remembered that he no longer had a career as a soldier. While he cursed the men who formed the Indian-uprising plan, he laid no blame on his present companions, for they took no part in his decision to desert and become a traitor.

Possibly only Jill knew how Marsden felt and of his fears for the future. As the days went by, it became a convention that Marsden helped Jill as much as his own duties allowed. The other men vied with each other to assist Liz with her horse management, but grinned, winked and stood aside to let Marsden lend Jill a hand.

"Tell you one thing, Jackson," Jill remarked on the evening of the third day as they stood by the horses and watched Liz hobble slowly towards the camp. "That Yankee gal's got guts."

"So have you," he answered.

"I'm doing it for the South," Jill told him. "If those yahoos stir up the Indians, the Yankees might win the War."

Suddenly Jill became aware of a slight tension come over the young man at her side. Seeing him glance down at the trail-dirty Union-blue sleeve of his jacket, she realised what her words meant to him. By his actions he had given up his career and ruined himself. Now she stood like a damned fool, rubbing salt in his open wounds. Contrition flooded over her. Reaching for his hand, she led him from sight of the camp. They came to halt in a depression which hid them from view. Turning to face Marsden, Jill looked up at his unshaven face.

"Lordy, Jackson," she said. "I'm sorry for what I just said——"

His hands found hers, clasping them and drawing her to him, feeling the warmth of her body against his. Next moment they were in each other's arms.

"It's no good!" Marsden moaned, trying to free himself.

"Why?" asked Jill, drawing back. "Because I'm a reb and you're——"

"Because I've no future. Nothing to offer you."

"And if I tell you I don't care?"

"They'll court martial me when I go back, Jill," Marsden tried to explain, reading the anger that grew in her eyes. "I'll be broken even if they don't have me shot as a deserter and traitor."

"You don't have to go back," Jill pointed out.

"I have to, Jill."

"Why?" she insisted.

"I took an oath at West Point and broke it. I have to go back when this is over."

"And what about me?" she asked, her voice brittle.

"Jill!" Marsden groaned. "I just have to go back."

"To the Yankees?"

"To my people."

Jill tore herself from his hands, glaring her fury at him. In her pent-up emotional state it seemed that he had tried to take advantage of her. She blamed him for making her forget the reason she hated the Yankees and turned her fury on him.

"You lousy *Yankee!*" she spat, then turned and fled back to the camp.

Black despair welled over Marsden as he watched the girl go. Suddenly he knew just how much Jill had come to mean to him. He wanted Jill to be his wife, loved her for her many good qualities, wished to share his life with her. Only he could offer her no life.

Dropping his hand, Marsden opened the flap of his holster and curled his fingers around the butt of the Colt.

"That's no way out, Jack!" Dusty's voice warned from behind him.

Turning, Marsden saw the small captain walking towards him and growled, "Did you——"

"By accident. I'd been taking a scout around and came back at the end of it. You're too much of a man to take that way out—even without what it would do to the girl."

"I've nothing to go on for."

"It's your decision," Dusty said calmly. "One thing though, Jack. Don't rush it."

With that Dusty swung around and walked towards the camp. Marsden stood for a long time before he angrily thrust down the Colt, closed the holster flap and followed on Dusty's heels.

If anybody at the camp noticed a change in Jill and

Marsden's attitude, they made no comment. Watching the girl, Marsden wanted to go to her, tell her he would stay in the South. Pride and his sense of duty prevented him from doing so. For her part, Jill also wanted to apologise, to beg Marsden's forgiveness, yet she, too, had a stubborn streak of pride. If either one had made the slightest move towards the other, they would have been plunged into a sea of reconciliation—only neither offered to make the move. So they sat silent, morose and letting the rift between them grow wider and wider.

Possibly Dusty would have tried to mediate, to bring Jill and Marsden back together, but he had much on his mind. He never continued marching until the sun set but always called a halt while enough light remained for his party to see their way to tending to the stock. How successful the policy proved showed in the excellent condition of the horses. While a little thinner, all still looked in fine shape and showed no signs of weakness.

Following their usual routine, the senior non-coms gathered around Dusty as he unfolded his map to calculate their day's journey and mark off the ever-decreasing distance to the ring drawn around the Salt and Clear Forks of the Brazos. Usually Marsden would have been in the group, but that night he sat in black despair by the fire which Jill, again following routine, built ready for preparing a meal. None of the men noticed that for once Liz lay awake and watched them, listening to every word they said.

"We'll be about here, I'd say," Dusty stated, tapping the map. "Put the Sulphur behind us this afternoon. Ought to cross the Sabine around noon tomorrow and be on the East Trinity the day after. I'd say four more days ought to see us in the area."

"Just thought, Cap'n," Ysabel put in. "The Deacon runs a spread on the East Trinity, ranch, supply house and store."

"Whereabouts?" asked Dusty.

"I'm not sure," Ysable admitted. "Only heard him talk about it."

"They might have called in there, Cap'n," Billy Jack suggested.

"Might," admitted Dusty. "If we see any sign of the place, and it's not too far off our line, we'll scout it. If not, we push on. I don't reckon we can start hoping for much until we cross the West Fork of the Brazos, but we'll expect it after the Denton."

"And if we haven't called the play right, Cap'n?" asked Billy Jack, never one to look on the bright side.

"I'm trying not to think about that," Dusty answered, trying to sound as if the responsibility sat lightly on his shoulders. "If we're wrong, there'll be a couple of Indian prophets without honour in their country. Here, put the maps in your saddlebags for me, Billy Jack. Kiowa, let's give the stock a last look over before dark. Sam, take Mr. Marsden and see what you can scare up between you for supper. Miss Dodd, make the coffee, please."

Watching the man go about their duties, Liz wished that she felt less tired and could raise the energy to try to lay hands on the map. Even now she did not know their destination and guessed that the map would tell her that. Perhaps if she could destroy the map, she could——Still thinking on that line she drifted off to sleep.

At dawn Liz awoke to a feeling of difference and for almost a minute could not think what brought about the change. Then she realised that the nagging stiffness which usually accompanied her waking had gone. She wanted to leap from the blankets, dance, throw cartwheels like a kid. Only the thought of what her relief from stiffness meant prevented her from displaying her pleasure. She could now go ahead with her plans for disrupting the party.

However, the chance to obtain the map did not present itself and Liz could not think of any other move. Before breakfast finished, she could see that the men knew of her improved condition. Even if she had not seen it at breakfast, Liz knew it later, for Dusty pushed on at a better speed.

The party crossed the Sabine River more than an hour before noon and kept up a good pace. At two o'clock in the afternoon, Liz rode between Jill and Billy Jack wondering if she might manage to get the plans that night, or if she could stir up some other kind of trouble. Maybe she could take advantage of the rivalry shown by the non-coms when helping her to set them at each other's throats? Or she might exploit the obvious differences which caused Jill and Marsden to quarrel.

Ahead of them, the ground dropped away in a steep slope and they steered a course to take them along its top. All around lay the open, rolling land Liz had come so used to seeing. She wondered what would happen to her should she carry out a successful plot to prevent Dusty Fog carrying out his orders.

As if in answer to Liz's thoughts, something went 'splat!' against her left ear and a spurt of dirt erupted from the ground ahead of her horse. She had never heard the sound of a close-passing bullet. The others all knew the sound, even without the following crack of a rifle, and all started to swing around to see who shot at them.

CHAPTER ELEVEN

They're Only Lousy Rebs

Sam Ysabel brought his huge roan around in a rump-scraping, dime-small pivot turn that would have made a British polo player's eyes sparkle in admiration; and he did it by heel pressure alone, his hands being occupied by transferring the Sharps rifle from crook of arm to butt-cuddled against his shoulder.

Even as Liz saw the line of blue-uniformed figures on the top of a slope some three hundred yards away, recognising them as salvation and the means to end the Texans' mission, she heard the bellow of Ysabel's rifle. Up on the slope, the firer of the first shot slammed backwards under the impact of Ysabel's .52 calibre bullet and flopped limply to the ground.

A wild yell, like the sound of hounds clamouring around a treed cougar, rang out from the Union troops. Yelling an order to charge, their leader sent them boiling down the slope in a wild rush; but he did not take the lead as one might expect. Instead it seemed that that he allowed as many of his party as possible to come between himself and those gun-handy Texans before allowing his horse to move forward.

Elation, pleasure—and just a touch of disappointment—filled Liz as she watched the soldiers charging down. Soon she would be among her own kind again and able to tell them all she knew of Dusty Fog's mission. Yet in a way she would miss the cheerful, uncomplaining companionship of the Texans, for she had found herself growing to like them despite her political feelings. She expected the Texans to dismount and make a fight and realised that she might be in the thick of flying lead very soon, but the thought did not frighten her.

"Scatter!" Dusty yelled, almost as an echo to Ysabel's shot.

Only Liz of the party did not know what the order meant. When laying his plans for the journey, Dusty prepared his men for just such an emergency. Having no intention of risking the success of his mission by fighting a superior-numbered enemy force if he could avoid it, he had planned accordingly. On his command, the party dissolved into fast-moving, fanning-out segments. Leading one pack horse, Billy Jack started his mount running along the top of the slope, with Jill at his side. Marsden gave the girl one piteous glance before urging his sorrel and a pack horse off on the heels of Kiowa's running black and Kiowa led the third pack horse as they cut off to the right. Swinging down his rifle, Ysabel brought the roan about in a half turn and set it galloping at an angle to Kiowa's right, going away from the Texan. Last to leave the field, Dusty headed his black stallion towards the slope. Even as he went, Dusty saw Liz following Billy Jack's section and wondered what game the girl played this time.

Liz's original movement after the others was involuntary. Used to travelling with the rest, her mare obeyed it herd-instinct and lunged forward on the heels of the departing horses. Even as she reached down on the reins, meaning to halt her mare and join her approaching companions-in-arms, a thought struck Liz. Clearly the Confederates did not intend to make a fight, and with that much of a lead they ought to be able to out-ride those clumsy-looking Union soldiers. So if she could only delay the rebels, her people might take them. At that moment Liz remembered the maps Billy Jack carried. They might be of the greatest help in locating the remainder of the Texans in case of an escape.

Eagerly she urged her mare after Billy Jack and Jill. The little mare proved to be a flier. Carrying less weight, and unencumbered by a trailing pack horse, Liz's mount closed up to and came between Billy Jack and Jill's. Then she started to edge her mare towards the pack horse which in turn moved in against Billy Jack's black and urged it towards the edge of the slope.

"Get over, J——!" Billy Jack started to yell, turning his head. The words trailed off as he saw Liz, not Jill, at his side.

When making arrangements for Jill's inclusion in the escape groups, Dusty had not included Liz. Should the party separate, it would be because they met a Yankee force among whom Liz, as a Union supporter, could be safely left. So Billy Jack felt a momentary surprise at seeing Liz. Then he guessed what she aimed to do. His black's hooves churned the earth on the very start of the slope. If it once went over, he knew it would stumble or be forced to slow down to such an extent that he fell into the hands of the Yankees.

Liz read the expression on the lean non-com's face and felt disgusted with herself. Thinking back to all the little kindnesses shown by her Billy Jack, she hated to be acting in such a treacherous manner. A few more inches would see him go over the edge of the slope—only she could not make herself continue. Before she could swing the mare clear, Liz felt her hat sent spinning from her head and two hands dug into her hair from behind, pulling at it, dragging her backwards out of the saddle. Her horse lost stride, a shriek of pain burst from her lips, then Billy Jack passed her and his black swung away from the edge of the slope.

"Keep going, Billy Jack!" screamed Jill's voice from close behind Liz.

On seeing Liz's attempt to ride Billy Jack off the level ground, Jill wasted no time. She urged her buckskin closer to the other two, leaning over to send Liz's hat flying, then lay hold of her hair. Billy Jack turned slightly in his saddle and saw the girls' horses slowing down. Even without Jill's advice, he would not have stopped, for he knew Dusty's orders on the subject. On hearing of Dusty's plans for such a situation, Jill agreed that she must be sacrificed rather than endanger her escort and stated that she would be reasonably safe in Union hands provided she knew nothing of the Texans' plans. So Billy Jack kept his horse running, the pack animal keeping pace at its side, and left Jill behind.

While holding rank as captain, and serving in a regiment which saw considerable action, Marty Levin had so far avoided contact—and its risks—with the enemy. Like most of his kind, he boasted that the rebels might be brave enough when bullying some poor negro, but showed a great lack of courage when faced with armed Union men. However, he never really believed that theory and expected a stiff fight on sighting his quarry. With that thought in mind, Levin made sure that he let his men lead the charge on the Texans. Much to his surprise, he saw the rebels separate into fleeing groups after one of their number shot down the guide who brought the party overland from the Red River.

"Split up!" he yelled wildly. "Get after them, Kill 'em!"

Although his men felt the exhilaration of the chase and the heady joy which came from the sight of the fleeing enemy, obeying Levin's order did not come easy. Members of Marsden's Zouave regiment, they had been formed into a mounted company in an attempt to answer the mobility of the Texas Light Cavalry; but they lacked the Texans' experience on horseback. Showing none of the Texans' rapid disintegration, Levin's company split apart and one group took out after each segment of Dusty's party. Due to lack of foresight and planning, Levin found himself with his sergeant, a burly, sullen hard-case called Fitch, and only two men. Taking the easiest course, he led his small group down with the intention of pursuing the girls and Billy Jack.

Levin's party watched Jill tackle Liz and the girls go sliding from their horses to the ground where they tangled in a wild-hair-tearing tangle of waving arms and thrashing legs. Instantly all thoughts of chasing Billy Jack were forgotten. The men slid their horses to a halt, laughing, whooping out encouragement and profane advice to the struggling girls. Bringing his mount to a sliding halt, Levin looked back.

"Get after hi——" he began.

The words died off as he recognised one of the fighting girls. Even through the trail-dirt and dishevelled coating, Levin made out the features of Liz Chamberlain. He wasted no time in wondering how she came to be involved in a hair-yanking brawl with another girl on the North Texas plains. Remembering that her father had considerable influence, both financially and politically, he reluctantly decided he must end what looked like developing into a promising fight.

"Pull them apart, Sergeant!" he ordered.

A scowl came to Fitch's face at the words, then he grinned and dropped out of his saddle. Moving forward, he watched the girls struggle to their knees still clinging to each other's hair, then grabbed Liz by the arms from behind. One of his men had also dismounted and caught Jill in a similar manner. Pulling backwards, the men managed to separate the girls, but it took all their strength to prevent a resumption of hostilities. Liz stopped struggling first and stood with face flushed and breasts heaving as she stared at her rescuers.

"Quit it, gal!" the soldier holding Jill yelled, and shook her hard.

Sanity returned to Jill, warning her of the futility of struggling. She relaxed and stood gasping for breath, glaring defiantly at Levin as he swung out of his saddle.

"Are you all right, Liz?" he asked.

Liz looked at the medium-sized, sallow-faced young man and found difficulty in recognising him. Not because he looked much different from her last meeting. Levin never looked clean or tidy even when in full dress, but because she had met so many people on her visit to Arkansas.

"I'll live," she replied, touching her left eye with a finger tip and wincing.

"What're you doing here? Who's that girl?"

"Her name's Jill Dodd," Liz answered guardedly.

"A rebel?" growled Levin.

"Yes, I am!" Jill put in, shrugging the man's hands from her and glancing hopefully towards the buckskin which had come to a halt some yards away.

"We'll take her along with us," Levin stated and looked to where Billy Jack faded off into the distance. "There's no chance of catching him now, Sergeant. We'll go on to the Deacon's place. The guide told me how to find it last night."

"Do your men know where to find you?" Liz inquired, as the second private rode after her mare and the buckskin.

"Yes," replied Levin—a slight pause which made Liz eye him suspiciously. Wanting to take her mind off the subject, he pointed to where Jill's Tranter lay on the ground. "We'd better take that with us."

The man behind Jill grabbed her again as she started to move forward and Liz went to pick up the revolver. Thrusting the Tranter into her waistband, she smiled at Jill.

"I'll return it when we part, reb," Liz promised.

"That's a good hoss," Fitch growled, eyeing the buckskin avariciously. "Too good for a rebel slut to—"

"He's too much horse for you, Yankee," Jill spat back.

"Yeah?" the sergeant grinned. "Well, I'll—"

"Take your own horse, Sergeant!" Liz ordered coldly.

Turning his eyes towards the girl, Fitch prepared to snarl a refusal. However, Levin backed Liz with his own command and Fitch slouched to his leg-weary mount.

On moving out, Jill strained her ears for sounds of shooting that would mean the Yankees had caught up with her friends. She heard nothing and concluded that the rest of the party must have made good their escape. Not that it surprised her when she came to consider the poor condition of the Yankee horses and inexperience of the captain.

Just how ignorant Levin was showed in the fact that he never once offered to dismount and walk to rest his horses. Riding on at a slow trot, he led his party due west. During the ride Liz learned what brought Levin to Texas. Although he approved of Castle's plan in theory, it contained too much danger for his liking. So he contented himself with commanding the escort to the Red River. After seeing the arms and Ager gun over into Texas, Levin prepared to make a fast ride to the safety of his own lines. On his way back, the civilian guide met him with orders from Colonel Stedloe. Marsden had deserted, taking news to the rebels. Guessing what Ole Devil Hardin would do, Stedloe sent orders for Levin to follow Castle's party and use his company to protect it. Instead of following the wagon tracks of Castle's party, the guide led them towards the Deacon's ranch; he showed as much reluctance as Levin had to going into the Indian council area. Fate intervened, bringing them into contact with the enemy and Levin considered his duty well done.

Night had fallen when the party rode towards the deserted ranch buildings. Being Eastern-raised, Levin had the horses taken into the barn instead of using the corral. Only

Liz's example made the men care for their horses before going to the ranch house in search of food. However, nothing Liz could do prevented Levin from locking Jill in a small saddlery-store in the barn. He said it was to keep her out of the men's way, but Liz suspected that Levin had the blind bigoted hatred all his kind showed towards the Southerners and so he merely took spite on the girl.

"I'll have food sent to you, reb," Liz promised and even managed a smile as she looked at the other's dirty face. "And I'll send along some hot water and soap."

"You need it yourself." Jill answered, eyeing Liz's unkempt appearance, now blackened eye, but unable to hold any hate against such a game girl.

However, when the door closed, Jill looked around her prison and felt like crying. The room was small, its walls stout and the window heavily barred—to keep out marauding black bears rather than prevent a prisoner escaping, but too strong for her to attempt anything against.

Time dragged by, Liz came with hot water, soap, a towel and Jill's other clothing, standing by while the rebel girl washed and changed.

"I'll bring you some food as soon as I can," Liz told Jill as she prepared to leave the room. "And we'll return you to your people first chance we get."

"Bring that lamp out with you," Levin called from the barn. "She might try to use it to burn her way out."

Figuring that Jill just might make such an attempt, Liz picked up the lamp and carried it out of the room. Left alone, Jill made herself as comfortable as possible and sat thinking of the past few days. A chink of light showed under the bottom of the door, for Liz insisted on leaving the barn well illuminated to help guide any of Levin's men who might be in the vicinity.

Time dragged slowly by. Outside the room, the horses in their stalls moved restlessly, chomping hay or stamping their hooves. Jill felt very tired and decided to try to settle down and sleep. Then she heard steps approaching the door, heavy and uneven-sounding steps which worried her. The lock clicked and the door jerked open. Leaning against the door's jamb, his face twisted in the slobber-lipped sneer of a bad drunk, Fitch looked Jill up and down.

"Come on out'f it, gal," he ordered in a whisky-slurred voice. "Me 'n' you's going to have some fun."

As he often received visitors who did not wish to discuss their business in the presence of the hired help, the Deacon lived in a small, one-room cabin separated by several yards from the bunkhouse. Levin and Liz sat at the table in the room, having just finished a meal she made for them. Although Liz wished to go and feed Jill, the man insisted on talking. Liz felt concerned for, on taking a meal to the soldiers, she learned that Fitch had found a couple of jugs of corn liquor. The men all appeared to have taken their share of the potent stuff, but Levin made no attempt to halt their excesses. Guessing he had made a mistake in the girl's eyes, Levin sought to divert her by discussing the business which brought him to Texas.

"Things could go bad wrong if the Texans escape and catch up with Castle," Liz remarked, after explaining her presence in Texas and telling all she knew.

"Yes," Levin agreed and, wishing to exculpate himself, went on, "I could've commanded the chase if I didn't have to stop and look after you. But you know what ignorant fools these men are."

Ignoring the latter part of Levin's speech, Liz warned, "I've an idea that Captain Fog knows the rendezvous."

"He can't. Why not even I know that for certain. Only the Deacon and Castle know where they're meeting the Indians. We didn't let any of the regulars know, so Marsden couldn't have told the rebels that. I always knew we couldn't trust those lousy regulars."

"Jack Marsden claimed he deserted because the scheme endangered thousands of innocent lives. Is that true?"

"No!" Levin spat out.

"But all the Texans seemed to be so sincere, and two of

them have lived amongst the Indians. They say that the braves will attack indiscriminately, killing civilians, women, children—"

"So?" growled the captain. "They're only lousy rebs."

For the first time Liz began to gain an inkling of the mentality of men like Levin. While preaching tolerance, his kind were capable of the most vicious, bigoted intolerance against anybody who did not blindly fall in with their way of thinking or follow their beliefs.

"But if there is dan—" Liz began.

Her words chopped off as she heard a shrill scream from the barn. Instantly Liz forgot her argument. Turning, she dashed across the room, tore open the door and raced towards the open doors of the barn. Levin followed on her heels, catching up with her just as she reached the barn's door. Both halted, looking to where Fitch held Jill pressed against the side of a stall, his hands tearing open the struggling girl's shirt front.

Only for a moment did Liz wait for Levin to order his sergeant away from the other girl. Levin made no such attempt, fearing to push a point where he might have to clash with his sergeant. True, Levin had behind him all the might and weight of the *Manual of Field Regulations*—and did not hesitate to use its powers in an area where backing waited to enforce his will. However, he knew that he possessed no such backing in Texas and must stand on his own feet. So he reclined to interfere when Fitch, noted as mean when wet, might refuse to obey him.

"Leave her be, Sergeant!" Liz shouted. "Make him, Levin!"

Twisting his leering face towards his superior officer, Fitch gritted, "All right, Levin, make me."

Fury etched itself on Levin's face and his right hand went to the hilt of the straight infantry sword he wore. He lacked the courage to draw the weapon, even though his sergeant no longer wore a weapon belt.

Liz sprang forward, drawing Jill's Tranter from her

waistband—and thanking the Lord that she had not put the gun aside when she changed.

"Let go, right now!" she hissed.

Something in her voice brought Fitch's eyes to her. What he read on her face caused him to release Jill, letting her fall sobbing against the wall. For a moment Fitch stood scowling uneasy defiance, but he could not meet the scorn and fury in the girl's level stare. Letting out a lurid curse, Fitch turned and slouched out of the barn.

"I'll deal with him in the morning," Levin promised, his voice a shade weak.

"Will you?" sniffed Liz and went to Jill's side.

Watching Fitch fade off into the darkness, Levin felt a sense of inadequacy at Liz having done something beyond his power to achieve. For Levin to know that someone could better him brought hatred against the one who did better. However, he felt it would be imprudent to show his hatred openly to Liz, so turned it against Jill instead.

"Maybe she knows where the rebs plan to meet up again after scattering," he said, pushing by Liz and tilting Jill's face upwards by gripping her chin. "Do you know, reb?"

Jill found herself faced with a different situation, one which did not scare her as much as the threat of rape by a drunken brute. So she kept quiet. Levin shook her head from side to side savagely.

"Where'll they meet?" he yelled.

"Go to hell!" Jill answered.

Viciously Levin swung his other hand, lashing it forward then back across Jill's face and rocking her head from side to side. Again he repeated the demand for information and received the same reply.

"That's enough!" Liz shouted.

Mean-minded and untrustworthy himself, Levin imagined everybody to be cut in the same mould. Suspicion came easily to him and he saw danger in Liz's words. Without giving any warning, he swung around and slapped the Tranter from her hand, then thrust her aside. Turning back to Jill, he lashed another slap across her face. Dazed by the blows and previous rough handling, Jill collapsed to her knees. Levin loomed above her, his sallow face contorted with fury and sadistic delight at inflicting pain.

"Where are those stinking rebs?" he almost screamed, and when no answer came from the girl, drew back his foot.

CHAPTER TWELVE

Come On, Brave Man—Try Me!

A heave, a scrabbling of hooves, then Dusty Fog and his black stallion made the top of the steep ridge. Turning, Dusty looked down and back to where a quarter of a mile away his pursuers urged their leg-weary, jaded horses after him. From the look of the long Springfield rifles slung across their shoulders, he judged them to be mounted infantry. In the Union Army even the volunteer cavalry outfits were armed with much shorter carbines of one kind or other. By the way the men sat their horses, he reckoned they would be unable to make the difficult climb which he had just accomplished. After leading them a chase of five miles, he decided that it was time he lost them anyway and went about his business.

Although he could have ridden clear away from his pursuers in less than a mile, Dusty held his black down to a pace which kept the Yankees believing they would overtake him at any moment, while leading them further and further away from their companions. At first the state of the land drove them south-east, but at last he began to make a long, looping half circle towards the west and now he headed in the right direction again.

Unshipping his Springfield and bringing his horse to a halt, one of the soldiers aimed and fired a shot. Where the bullet went was anybody's guess, but it came nowhere near Dusty. Grinning, the small Texan drew back a little from the rim and flattened down to offer a smaller target while watching the Yankees approach the foot of the slope. The corporal in charge of the section started to urge his horse up the slope and although the animal responded gamely, it could make no headway. Nor did any of the others do better.

"Here endeth the first lesson," mused Dusty and slipped back from the rim. "I don't reckon they'll bother me again."

Returning to the stallion, Dusty took the reins and started to walk. He led the horse for some way until he found an area which offered him shelter from unfriendly eyes. At the foot of a bush-dotted valley, he stripped off the black's saddle and allowed the horse to roll while preparing to water and feed it.

When the horse had cooled down from its exertions, Dusty took his canteen and tipped the contents into his hat's crown. Taking the bit from its mouth, he allowed the horse to drink its fill. With that done, he unpacked the nosebag from the saddlepouch ready to start feeding. One of the reasons Dusty did not bring carbines on the mission had been because the weapon's boot made an ideal receptacle for an emergency feed of grain. Tipping the golden drops of concentrated energy from the boot into the nosebag, he set up the stallion with a better feed than he himself would have until he joined up with the rest of his party. While the black first ate its grain, then grazed on the ankle-deep buffalo grass, Dusty watched his back trail. He saw no sign of the Union soldiers, nor did he expect to.

An hour later Dusty rode on again. Although he kept constantly alert, he saw nothing of friend or foe. That did not surprise him, for he knew his men would scatter far across the range and lead their hunters as he had done. The Yankee officer in command of the company was going to have the hell of a chore rounding up his men again when the Texans finally shook them off.

Although he never cared to risk his horse by riding in darkness, Dusty kept going for a time after night fell. In this he was helped by the fact that the big black stallion showed considerable skill at traveling in the darkness. He believed himself to be safe from any pursuit, but wished to cover as many miles as possible towards the rendezvous with his men. Using the instinct gained during a lifetime on the great Texas ranges, and steering his course by the stars, Dusty continued to move towards the west.

Topping a rim, he saw lights down to his left. A small ranch's buildings, he guessed. Maybe the Deacon's place near the East Trinity. If not, Dusty stood a better than fair chance of finding Confederate supporters at the buildings. Possibly one or more of his party might be present.

With the possibility of the place belonging to the Deacon, Dusty did not ride blindly and noisily towards the buildings. He saw no sign of life around the place, apart from the lights in the barn and showing from windows of two of the other buildings. Nor could he see horses in the corrals.

Dusty was still almost a quarter of a mile from the buildings when he heard a girl's terrified scream ring out. Almost without conscious thought, Dusty drew his left-hand Colt, clicking back the hammer under his thumb. Even as he prepared to put spurs to the black's flanks, he saw the front door of one building jerk open. Liz burst into sight, racing towards the barn and behind her squinted a Union Army officer. Watching the girl and Levin dash into the barn, Dusty felt concern for the welfare of Billy Jack and Jill. Maybe his loyal sergeant-major had been killed or captured. He decided to move in on foot. If Billy Jack was held prisoner, then he must be rescued. If not, well the fates would take care of things from then on.

Before Dusty could dismount, he saw a burly sergeant leave the barn. From the way the man walked, Dusty figured him to be toting a fair load of corn liquor. It did not require the second-sight of a Comanche witch-man to guess at the cause of Jill's screams. Dusty hoped that Liz arrived in time to save Jill from the drunken Yankee.

The presence of the Yankee officer hinted at there being a Union force on hand, or at least an escort. Knowing how he would act under similar circumstances, spending a night in hostile territory, Dusty thought there might be sentries posted around the place. He reached the corral without any alarm being given and prepared for a dash towards the barn. Looping the black's reins over the corral rail, Dusty found his eyes on the sabre. If the Yankee had guards out, he must deal with them silently. Cold steel made a mighty effective silencer. While the 1860 Army Colt might be as fine a revolver as made to that date, it lacked the more robust qualities which made its descendants—particularly the 1873 Model P Peacemaker or the 1911 Government Model automatic pistol—such handy clubs when empty. Striking a blow with the barrel of the Army Colt could only be done with the serious risk of snapping the loading lever's retaining catch, or damaging the cylinder which, unlike fitted on later models, had no top strap covering and protecting it. The Haiman sabre had no such defects. A blow from its hilt would stun a man, while a thrust of its point to the kidney area was certain to drop a man in such agony that he would be unable to cry out in a few seconds of life left to him.

Drawing the sabre, having holstered his Colt earlier, Dusty darted across the open space. Voices came from the barn. Shouted demands for information in a male voice. Dusty also heard Jill make some answer, then the sound of slaps and more yelled questions. Just as Dusty burst into the barn, he saw Levin slap the Tranter from Liz's hand, then turn to shout at Jill.

"Where're those stinking rebels?" Levin screeched, drawing back his foot for a kick.

"Right here," Dusty told him.

Letting out a startled yelp, lowering his foot hurriedly and turning, Levin swung around to face Dusty. For a moment Levin's hands quivered ready to rise in surrender, then he saw that Dusty appeared to be alone and held a sabre instead of a Colt.

During his time in college Levin had learned fencing. In fact he became very good with a blade, having found that such gave him access to the company of the rich students he hated for having more money than himself. Taking in Dusty's small size and apparent youth, Levin decided that victory would be certain enough for him to risk his valuable neck in a fight. Then he noticed the gunbelt and matched Colts and a momentary fear gripped him. However, he knew the chivalrous nature of the Southerners and doubted if the small Texan would draw a gun if challenged to fight with swords.

"You'd best surrender, reb," Levin warned. "If not I'll cut you down."

"Like you did to Jill?" asked Dusty. "Come on, brave man—try me!"

Something in Dusty's manner gave pause to Levin's actions. Levin tried to tell himself that he could not trust Dusty to fight fairly, but he knew that fear held him from making a move. Then he thought back to his college successes and decided he could risk a sword fight against the obviously much younger and smaller man, provided the other kept his guns out of it.

"You'd shoot me down if I tried," Levin sneered. "I'm not wearing a gun."

"That's a sword at your side," Dusty pointed out. "Pull it and use it. Only you'll find it harder than slapping a gal around."

Liz had darted to Jill's side and knelt by the rebel girl, arm around her. Looking up, Liz watched Levin draw his sword and ran the tip of her tongue across her lips. All too well she knew of his skill with the sword and wanted to warn Dusty, to give the small Texan a chance to make an escape. Before the words came out, she saw they would be too late.

Out slid Levin's sword, its thirty-four inch blade glinting under the barn's light. In height, weight and reach Levin held all the advantages. He looked forward to an easy victory; to killing the small Texan, for he had no intention of accepting a surrender. Perhaps his men would hear the noise and come to investigate. If so, he wanted them to see him killing or having killed, a rebel officer. Then those sullen, mutinous scum would be more amenable to his orders. He could arrest and punish Fitch for daring to show disrespect to him.

Studying the way Levin assumed the on-guard position, Dusty guessed that the other knew more than a little about the use of a sword and studied the Hungarian style of sabre work. Dusty favoured the French school, having learned fencing from a New Orleans master. As in everything he set his mind to, Dusty learned his fencing lessons well and kept up his practice by training with the other officers of the Texas Light Cavalry.

Up lifted Levin's sword blade in the first move of the salute. Immediately Dusty began a reply—and Levin changed from the salute to a vicious cut across at Dusty's exposed right side. Liz let out a low, angry gasp at the treacherous move, expecting to see Dusty go down with his ribs slit open.

Levin's move failed for one reason. From what he saw of the other, Dusty had not expected courtesy or fair play. So, while he replied to the salute, Dusty stayed alert for just such a move. In a smooth flicker, the Haiman's blade came down, engaged the foible of Levin's sword and deflected it. From where Dusty sent the point of the sabre licking out in a thrust. Only by making a hurried, unorthodox and startled leap to the rear did Levin avoid taking Dusty's point in the belly.

Catching his balance, Levin met Dusty's attack. If Levin expected to rely on his superior reach to keep Dusty back to a distance where the Texan's attacks depended solely upon ripostes, making an offensive action following a successful parry, he was disappointed. Instead of standing back, Dusty drove forward, fighting well within Levin's reach and cramping his prearranged moves. Levin knew how he would be fighting matched against a taller man and could not conceive that any brain might devise another method. In a very few passes he learned that Dusty did not intend to blindly follow his lead in the way they fought.

Liz and Jill stayed where they were, watching the fight. Of the two, Liz understood more fully the high standard of the sword-play shown by both men. After a few passes, Liz became lost to the true implications of the fight in studying the beauty and grace of the movements and the skill of the participants. Having seen a great many fencing matches, and knowing something of the game herself, Liz realised just how good both men were. Levin had speed, a devastatingly fast beat, could bind his opponent's blade and take it out of line, then make his own move, be it lunge, cut or feint, with startling rapidity. Yet for all that, Liz became slowly aware that Dusty was the superior man. It became clear that Dusty did not fluster in the face of speed. Dusty knew that speed alone could not assure success. In fact, on a couple of occasions Levin's speed almost brought him to grief when he made a very fast one-two attack and found his blade coming back into closed line from the second disengage before Dusty moved. Both times only Levin's skill saved him from a wound, but he knew that he had met his match with a sabre.

In desperation Levin changed styles, going in point first

as if handling a training foil or duelling sword. Instantly Dusty adopted the same method of fighting and, despite the sabre's awkwardness in such work, showed that he excelled in that form of fighting too. The master who instructed Dusty in fencing was a French-Creole and never considered the sabre to be a gentleman's weapon. One learned to use the sabre well, of course, and it did have uses in mounted warfare, but a gentleman much preferred the more artistic and skillful use of the point instead of slashing with a cutting edge. So the master insisted that his pupils became fully conversant with the finer points of sword work and again Dusty proved a most adept pupil.

Just how adept showed when Dusty began to drive the other back across the barn, the lightning fast point of his sabre coming time after time within a hair's-breadth of catching Levin's body. Once again the Yankee was forced to revert to a slashing attack. Desperation lent him the courage of a frightened rat and he launched an attack which forced Dusty to retire towards the door of the barn. Sweat poured down Levin's face and he found difficulty in breathing. Dusty, being fitter and in better condition, showed less signs of distress and knew that it would be only a matter of minutes before he could terminate the fight. However, he knew he might not be spared those minutes. At any moment the Yankee sentries might hear the sound of steel against steel and come to investigate.

Timing his moves just right, Dusty feinted to Levin's head in the start of a compound attack. Up rose Levin's arm in an attempted parry and too late he realised his mistake. At just the right moment Dusty's feint changed to its true purpose and came down in a cut at Levin's body. Shining steel glittered as it drove across to bite through Levin's clothing and inflict a painful gash in the man's side. Levin screeched like a stuck pig as the blade bit home. Although the wound was not serious, he dropped his sword and stumbled, backwards to fall against the wall of a stall. He hung there, eyes wild with fear and mouth opening to beg for mercy.

"Dusty, behind you!" Jill screamed.

Fitch had returned to the bunkhouse in a smouldering humour and found the two soldiers in that stage of drunkenness when they could be persuaded to take any kind of action. Setting to the task, he soon had the soldiers ready to go with him to the barn. Levin had never been popular with the men under him and neither objected to teaching him a lesson as a prelude to taking and having fun with the girl. Collecting their rifles, each man fitted on his bayonet as a means of quietening any objections. Levin might show. Then they headed for the barn. Fitch watched them go and a drunken sneer came to his face. Once they dealt with Levin, they would be mutineers and he had the right to kill them. After that the girls would be his until he chose to leave. He intended to show that officer's daughter where she came off, it ought to be fun.

Not until almost at the barn did the two soldiers realise anything was wrong. Neither had heard the clash of steel and did not recognise the sound. However, when they approached closer to the open doors, they saw Levin in the final stages of his fight. The sight of the cadet-gray uniform of Levin's attacker drove all thoughts of mutiny from their heads. Even as Dusty began his compound attack, the soldiers charged forward to help out their officer.

If they had come in side by side, making a concerted rush, the two men would have had Dusty at their mercy. In the heady exhilaration of the prospect of a fight, mingled with whisky consumption, they made a race of their attack and one proved fleeter of foot than the other.

Howling a wild shout, the first man launched a thrust at Dusty's body. He gave the small Texan no chance to use the sabre and only Dusty's swift-sidestep caused the blow to miss. Carried on by his own momentum, the soldier rushed forward. He felt a hand clamp hold of his shirt front, saw Dusty slipping backwards under him, contact with a boot that rammed into his belly. Then the soldier lost all knowledge of the subsequent happenings. He had a vague knowledge of losing his balance and felt the foot against his belly giving a powerful shove. Instantly the room appeared to whirl around and he saw the floor rushing towards him. The rifle clattered to the floor as Dusty performed the *tomoe-nage* stomach throw of ju jitsu and sent the soldier sailing into the air. Taken by surprise, with his reflexes slowed through the whisky-drinking, the soldier could do nothing to break his fall. Down he crashed, landing head first on the hard-packed earth floor of the barn. A dull pop sounded as the neck bones broke and the soldier's limp body crumpled to the ground.

By that time his companion had arrived. Roaring with rage, the second man raised his rifle and sent the bayonet driving down at Dusty's recumbent body. With a rolling twist of his hips, Dusty avoided the thrust and the bayonet's tip shattered on impact with the ground. Even while performing the *tomoe-nage* Dusty retained his grip on the sabre. Twisting back, he drove upwards in what would have been a thrust if aimed at the body. Instead the sabre passed between the man's legs and its razor-sharp blade sliced into the soft flesh of the inner thigh to sever the femoral artery. Blood followed the sabre from the gash in a rushing flood. The solider had but thirty seconds to live.

Dusty received no respite. Even as he started to rise, and while the stricken soldier lurched blindly away, Dusty saw yet another menace to his life. Still carrying the stone jug, Fitch arrived on the scene. With a snarl of rage, he sprang forward. Ignoring the gun at his belt, Fitch swung the jug around like a club and struck at the small Texan's head. Only just in time did Dusty duck. He had just made his feet and moved his head down quickly. The jug brushed Dusty's hat in passing and he took a fast pace to the rear before launching a backhand cut which laid open Fitch's belly like an axe-split melon. Fitch stumbled backwards, guts pouring out of the terrible wound. Behind Dusty, Liz screamed, covering her face with her hands to shut out the terrible sight.

While just as shocked and horrified as Liz, Jill saw something which made her forget, momentarily, the nausea which arose in her. Levin made no attempt to help his men at first, but stood cowering against the stall. Nor did the sight of the first two deaths effect him. Being entirely self-centered, like all his kind, Levin cared nothing for the men under him. All he knew was that he had a chance to save his own miserable life. On the ground not far from him lay Jill's Tranter and, while Dusty met Fitch's attack, Levin screwed up sufficient courage to go forward to grab the weapon. Knowing his lack of skill with a revolver, Levin moved forward, meaning to get so close that he could not miss.

Taking the scene in, Jill knew she must do something to save Dusty. Close at hand a pitchfork leaned against the wall. She had tried to reach it when Fitch made his rape attempt. Unhindered by other hands, she caught up the fork and sprang forward. Pure blind chance directed the prongs of the fork into just the right place, for Jill struck without conscious effort. Levin was just lining the revolver at Dusty's back when he felt a sudden, excruciating agony bite into him. Arching his back, Levin triggered off a wild shot. Dusty whirled around, sabre ready for use, and saw Levin crumpling forward. The Yankee crashed to the ground at Dusty's feet, the shaft of the pitchfork rising from his back. One glance told Dusty what caused the instant collapse. Either by design or accident, Jill sent its prongs into Levin's kidneys and ended his murder attempt.

Dusty knew he must waste no time. Although both girls appeared to be on the verge of hysterics, he had more important things on his mind. At any moment the rest of the Yankee party would arrive, attracted by the shot. He must be prepared to fight his way clear and make for the black. Could he leave Jill and Liz behind? Would they be safe in the hands of the leaderless party. From what Dusty had seen of the sergeant and soldiers, and smelled on their breaths, discipline must be lax. If the rest of the party had also been drinking, maybe not even Liz would be safe among them.

Thinking of the girls caused Dusty to look for their horses. Only four other mounts stood in the stalls alongside the buckskin and mare. Maybe the whole of the Yankee party lay around the barn. Dusty decided to take a chance on his guess proving correct.

Gently he led the girls from the barn and into the cool night air. Possibly because she had seen violent death more than once with the buckwhackers, or maybe because the victims were Yankees and not good specimens at that, Jill recovered control of herself before Liz regained a hold.

"Are there any more of them, Jill?" Dusty asked.

"Only those in the barn," she finally managed to answer. "I ki—"

"Easy, gal," Dusty put in as her words trailed off. "Let's get Miss Chamberlain to the house. Say, did they get Billy Jack?"

Jill caught Liz's eye and read pleading on the other girl's face. Neither of them knew for sure how Dusty would react when he heard of Liz's action. Possibly he might leave the Yankee girl behind when he rode on. Nothing Liz could think of would be worse than being left alone in that place of death. Jill realised that at last she had a Yankee almost pleading with her, silently begging for help.

"My horse stumbled, Captain," she stated. "I yelled to Billy Jack to keep going and he did, just as you ordered."

"Huh, huh," Dusty grunted. "You girls go up to the house. I'll do what I can in the barn. Make up a meal for me, please, Jill. We'll put out after we've rested."

CHAPTER THIRTEEN

This's What They'll Turn Loose

The East Trinity River lay almost an hour's ride behind Dusty Fog and the two girls. Overhead the sun began to dip down past its noon height. Up on a rim stood a magnificent specimen of longhorn Texas cattle. Big, black, nine hundred pounds of powerful frame, with a six foot spread of needlepointed horns capable of gutting a black bear or impaling a cougar gracing its head, a bull of the first water. Giving a deep-throated bellow, the bull swung around and passed over the rim from sight. Dusty brought his horse to a halt and a wistful grin twisted his lips.

"Whooee!" he said. "I bet he's a mean one. If the good Lord made anything more cross-grained, stubborn, ornery or vicious than a Texas longhorn, I sure've never seen it. One of 'em'll charge you after you've hauled it from a bog-hole; run a hoss ragged chasing it; hunt the worst cover it can find; damned near burst your teeth trying to chew its meat when it's dead. But it sure makes a real pretty sight when you've been away from home for a spell."

Liz stared at Dusty in surprise. After seeing him fight and watching the calm component, efficient manner he handled the problems of the march, she had thought him to be hard, dehumanised almost by the life war forced him to lead. Now she saw him in a different light. That coldly confident young man felt homesick and must be thinking of his folks, his home in the Rio Hondo country.

"Your family must have many slaves for you to give up so much, face such dangers, live such a life that you can keep them," she commented.

"There's no slaves in the Rio Hondo country, only a few coloured folks and they're all free."

"Then why did you—" Liz began.

"Come on now, Miss Chamberlain," Dusty interrupted with a smile. "You know that the slavery issue's only one reason the South fought. A mighty good one for the Yankees to use. It's making your soldiers feel mighty noble to believe they're fighting to free a lot of bad done-by slaves. Only most slaves live just as well as a white worker up north—and nobody's thought of what they aim to do with all the Negroes when they're set free."

"If Texas isn't a slave state, why did they fight?" Liz insisted.

"There are some slaves in Texas," Dusty admitted. "Down on the coast you'll find a few, but I don't think there're ten men in Texas who own enough slaves to need an overseer. Nope, slavery's not what brought Texas into the War."

"What then?" asked Liz.

"We figure that each State is a sovereign government. Fact being that idea goes right back to when the original thirteen States combined. The States formed to be of mutual benefit to each other. Way we see it, if our State doesn't like the way things are run, then it should be allowed to pull out."

"Cap'n Dusty's right on that," Jill asserted.

"Sure," Dusty said. "Another thing Texas didn't like

was the way the Union asked us to join, gave us promises, and then sold us down the river."

"How do you mean?" asked Liz.

"We were told to disband the Rangers and did it believing the Union would give us armed protection against the Indians and the Mexicans. That aid never came. It gave the Secessionists fuel to burn and they stirred up folks. Uncle Devil decided, and it wasn't an easy decision, that we fought for the South."

"And you don't believe in slavery?" Liz insisted.

"No, ma'am. Only I sure as hell can't see how throwing thousands of Negroes out into the world and telling them they're free folks will solve their problems. I read about riots in New York a few years back; white folks objecting to slaves sent north by the underground railroad* coming into town and grabbing their work. If—"

"Dusty!" Jill gasped, for the first time dropping the formal 'Captain' in her agitation and pointing ahead of them.

On following the direction of Jill's point, the discussion on the coloured people problem became forgotten. A puff of smoke rose into the air from the side of a distant hill, closely followed by two more.

"Indians?" Liz gasped.

"You might say that," grinned Dusty. "Sam Ysabel's as near to an Indian as a white man can come."

"I don't understand," Liz gasped.

"It's part of the plan we made for it we had to split up," Dusty answered. "I made no rendezvous. Told Sam Ysabel to out-ride his hunters, make sure he had a clear area around him and then send up smoke. The rest of the party gathered in on the smoke when they saw it."

"Then none of you but Sam could know where the others would gather," Liz said. "How about if he was caught?"

*Underground Railroad: Organisation for smuggling freed slaves to Northern States.

"If Kiowa hadn't seen Sam's smoke three hours after noon on the day after we split up, he was to send up the smoke. Only I didn't expect any trouble. I've yet to see Yankee calvary that can out-ride those boys of mine."

"No bunch as sorry mounted as that lot back there could," Jill stated.

"I'm sure. I saw a rider a moment ago," Liz interrupted. "Yes. There. Look!"

Turning their eyes, Dusty and Jill saw a distant rider. The girls could see nothing more than that, but Dusty grinned and said, "Billy Jack."

Almost as if he heard the words, Billy Jack swept off his hat and waved it over his head. Instead of riding towards them in a straight line, however, Billy Jack continued forward, approaching the others on a diagonal course which also kept him headed on the required route to the west.

A momentary fear hit Liz as she watched the man approach them. No matter what Jill had told Dusty, Billy Jack knew the true reason for her capture by the Yankees. Nor would he be likely to forget Liz's attempt to ride him over the slope and deliver him into Union hands.

"See you get clear, Cap'n," Billy Jack remarked, although Liz felt his eyes studied her coldly.

"There's times I don't know how you get so smart and all-seeing, you old goat,"Dusty answered. "Have any trouble in shaking your lot?"

"I may as well tell you, Captain Fog," Liz put in stiffly. "I tried to get Sergeant-Major—" she paused as she could not remember ever hearing Billy Jack's surname. "I tried to cause the sergeant-major's capture. Jill stopped me and that was how she came to be in Union's hands."

"I sure hope the Yankees pulled you pair apart a mite gentler than we did," Dusty answered.

Two pairs of eyes turned to him as the meaning of Dusty's words struck the girls. Suddenly both realised that he must have seen everything before taking his horse over the top of the slope.

"Then you knew all along about Liz trying to have Billy Jack captured," Jill gasped.

"Saw some of it," agreed Dusty.

"Tell you though, Cap'n Dusty," Billy Jack put in. "Miss Liz was pulling her hoss back even before Jill jumped her."

"And she only did what I would've done in the same position," Jill went on.

"Reckon she did," Dusty grinned. "All right, swing down and let's start walking for a spell. That is unless Miss Chamberlain figures to sit down for a spell."

"I tried *that,*" Liz reminded him. "It didn't work then and I doubt if it would now."

"How did your lot go, Billy Jack?" asked Dusty as they started walking.

"Easy enough. I could've rid them out of sight in less than a mile, but I allowed to give 'em some work to do. Lost them in some rough country down south a piece. Say, how come you tied in with the girls?"

Dusty explained and Billy Jack listened with a grin. A wistful gleam came into the sergeant-major's eyes when Dusty mentioned tangling with the Yankee captain and Billy Jack promised himself that he would hear the full story from one of the girls as his captain gave only the bare details and omitted any reference to either his duel with Levin or battle against the other members of the enemy party. All Dusty mentioned was that he tangled with the Yankees, then after a meal left the ranch; neither girl wished to stay there through the night with the bodies in the barn. After covering a couple of miles from the Deacon's place, Dusty and the girls camped for the night and moved on at dawn.

Alert and watchful, the party continued to head west. They made their way towards the hill from which the smoke rose, although after the brief puffs no sign of human life showed. For all any of the party saw, they might have been the only people in the whole of the North Texas range country. While approaching the hill, they saw no hint of Sam Ysabel's presence and Liz, for one, wondered if some hitch had come to Dusty's arrangements. Barely had the doubt come than Ysabel rose from cover behind a large rock. Rifle across his arm as usual, he came down the slope and for once his impassive face showed emotion. Grinning his relief, he advanced towards the others.

"Howdy, Cap'n, folks," he greeted. "See you made it."

"Looks that way," Dusty agreed, also grinning. "You alone here?"

"Sure. Likely Kiowa's got his-self all lost. Them Kiowas never could find their way around."

"Have any trouble shaking your bunch?" asked Dusty.

"Nope. I took off a way and lost 'em in some cedar brakes down thataways. I reckon they're still lost. Been here sooner, but my roan threw a shoe."

"Isn't there any sign of Ja—Kiowa yet?" Jill put in.

"Why not say 'Jackson,' reb?" Liz interjected. "It'll be as easy and we all know who you mean."

A red flush crept into Jill's cheeks and she glared at Liz, but her concern for Marsden's welfare prevented her from making any comment. Instead she turned and looked expectantly at the big sergeant with pleading in her eyes.

"None I've seen," admitted Ysabel. "Let's get the hosses out of sight. And don't you worry none, gal, he'll show up real soon."

Turning, Ysabel walked off and the others followed him to a pleasant, well-concealed valley with the small stream meandering along its bottom. The roan and pack horse stood grazing on the stream's bank and Dusty told his party to off-saddle and rest their mounts.

"I'll go back and keep watch, Cap'n," Ysabel suggested. "Haven't seen any sign of Injuns, but they do say that's the time to watch out for 'em."

"So I've heard," Dusty drawled. "Only you'd best come back and lend us a hand with the shoeing. That damned roan's got meanness in him."

Ysabel gave out with a deep cough of laughter. "If you reckon the roan's mean, you should see my boy Loncey's white. That old Nigger hoss of his makes my roan look as peaceable as a preacher at a ladies' sewing-bee."

Although Dusty thought that Ysabel exaggerated a mite, the day would come when he saw the truth of the big sergeant's words.

Billy Jack finished tending to his horse and turned to go towards the pack animal. However, Jill turned from her buckskin and called, "Just get the pack off, Liz and I'll see to the horse while you handle the shoeing."

While seeing that the suggestion would save time, Billy Jack wondered if he could trust Liz not to try further delaying tactics. Liz saw his hesitation and made a quick decision. Walking to Billy Jack, she looked him straight in the face.

"I'll give you my word that I won't make any trouble," she said.

"That's good enough for me," he replied.

On opening the pack, Billy Jack struck a serious snag. He knew that Dusty planned to push on as soon as the shoeing was completed, leaving Kiowa to follow their tracks on his arrival at the rendezvous. So the discovery Billy Jack made did not please him and he doubted if it would make Dusty feel any delight.

"I can't start shoeing yet, Cap'n," the sergeant-major announced. "Got the buffer, drawing knife and rasp, but the shoeing-hammer and pincers are with Kiowa. Sam's pack hoss had the nails though and his shoes are in his saddle pouch."

"We'll just have to wait for Kiowa then," Dusty replied.

To do so meant a delay, but Dusty knew it was unavoidable. Every horse carried a set of ready-made shoes for just such an emergency, but replacing one called for the correct tools. When arranging the packs, Dusty had had to share out the loads equally between the three load-carrying horses. Shoeing equipment weighed far heavier for its bulk than did grain or human food, so he shared Billy Jack's kit among the three animals. The system failed due to the unforeseen circumstances of a horse throwing a shoe after the party split up for a time to avoid any enemy attack.

Listening to the men talk, Liz knew that a delay to their march had come. She should have been delighted, but somehow could not raise any pleasure at having her work done for her. Since listening to Levin's comment when she mentioned the danger to innocent civilians, she wondered if Castle's plan might be as ill-advised as the Texans claimed.

Dusty told the girls to grab some rest when they finished tending to the stock, then he left the valley and walked up to where Ysabel kept watch among the rocks. Looking across the range, Dusty could see no sign of Kiowa and Marsden.

"You say you've seen no sign of Indians, Sam," he said.

"Nary a sign, Cap'n."

"Is that good or bad?"

"Bad as a riled-up diamondback cornered in a barrel. Saw a big bunch of buffalo back a piece. Found signs that Indians had jumped 'em further on, couple of days back. Old men and squaws had done the killing."

"And?" Dusty prompted, although he could guess.

"Hunting's men's work. Only time they leave it to the squaws's when there's war-medicine in the air," Ysabel explained.

"That's what I figured," Dusty said quietly. "We could've called our guess at the council place right."

"Could have," agreed Ysabel.

"Wonder if Kiowa and Jack Marsden made it," Dusty remarked after a pause.

"If the bunch after 'em were no better mounted than them who took after me, ole Kiowa could out-ride 'em,"

Ysabel guessed. "And young Marsden rides real good—for a Yankee."

"Real good," agreed Dusty. "I don't like the delay though."

Not until shortly before sundown did Kiowa and Marsden make their appearance. Jill tried to stand back, act cold and distant, but failed. Giving a relieved gasp, she flung herself into Marsden's arms.

"Let's have the horses tended to," Dusty remarked.

"I'll see to Mr. Marsden's," Liz promised, "or the pack horse, whichever you want, Captain."

"The choice's your own, ma'am," Dusty told her with a grin. "How's that for Southern hospitality?"

Leaving Liz to handle Marsden's sorrel, Dusty helped Billy Jack to unload and unpack the pack horse's load. While waiting for Kiowa's arrival, Billy Jack had prepared the roan for being re-shod. Due to Dusty's foresight in having each horse fresh-shod before leaving the regiment, much of Billy Jack's work had been done and he only needed to ensure that the horn grown since the last shoeing be removed and the bearing surface for the reception of the new shoe made level by judicious use of the rasp. After that, he nailed a cold shoe into place and finished his work.

Knowing Billy Jack's skill in such matters, Dusty left him to his work and joined Kiowa at the fire. With the horses cared for, Liz knelt at the fire preparing a meal for the men. She listened to the conversation out of simple curiosity, not because she sought some information useful in spoiling Dusty's arrangements.

"Saw some Indian sign down to the south," Kiowa remarked. "Couple of sizeable bunches headed north-west. Then we came across a bunch of young Kaddo bucks and hid out from 'em. That's why we came in so late."

"Those Kaddos headed right for the council grounds?" asked Dusty.

"Reckon so," admitted the lean sergeant. "We called it right, Cap'n."

"Looks that way. Say, where's Jill and Jack Marsden?"

"Need you ask," smiled Liz.

"Reckon not," Dusty admitted with a grin. "Only I hope they don't stop out there spooning too long. We've some fast moving to do to make up for the delay."

Next day the party pushed on at a fast pace, riding and walking to such purpose that they made all of forty miles. Nor did they slow down the following day. The party crossed the Elm Fork of the Trinity just below its junction with the Denton and passed over the Trinity's West Fork so as to make camp on the southern tip of Lake Bridgeport. That night first the girls, then the men, grabbed a chance to swim in the lake, wash off the travel dirt and try to soak away the ache of hard travel. Dawn found them moving across what today is Jack County. Having found Indian sign, fresh and headed west, Dusty now kept Ysabel out ahead as scout and Kiowa brought up the rear. The rest of the party kept together, still traveling fast but now using caution and even more alert for trouble. Dusty no longer feared trouble from the Yankees, but he knew the Indians would be a far more serious menace than any Union soldiers.

"What are those?" Liz asked, pointing to several circling black dots in the noonday sky, as she walked at Dusty's side and led her mare.

"Turkey buzzards," he answered. "Hovering over an Indian kill, maybe." For all his light tone, Dusty gave the turkey vultures another glance before directing his gaze towards Ysabel. Seeing the sergeant halt, turn and wave, Dusty went on. "Mount up. Keep back a piece, you girls."

Leaving the other two men to guard the girls, Dusty urged his horse to a faster pace and joined Ysabel on top of a rolling fold of land. A low hiss of anger left Dusty's lips at what he saw below on the other side of the slope. Side by side, Dusty and Ysabel rode down the slope towards what had once been a peaceful, neat little cabin. When Dusty told Liz that the circling turkey vultures could be hovering over an Indian's kill, he meant a buffalo, elk, or maybe a longhorned butchered for meat. What lay before him was not so innocent.

By the corral lay the naked, mutilated shape of what had been a burly white man, the mangled flesh giving no hint as to which of the many holes and gashes killed him. Not far away the gutted body of a large dog sprawled in death.

"Why the hell do they have to carve a man up like that?" Dusty growled. "I wonder who he was."

"Dutchy Ritter, Cap'n," Ysabel replied. "I know his dawg. He was a horse-trader with a wife and two kids."

"When did it happen?"

"Towards evening yesterday, I'd say. Don't get it though. Dutchy allus got on with the Comanches and this's Comanche county."

Dusty did not reply. Riding to the house, he swung from his saddle and walked to the shattered door. Only by an effort could he force himself to enter the building, for he guessed what he would find inside. Through necessity Dusty had become accustomed to seeing death, but he was pale under his tan as he returned to the open again. He expected the sight in the room to be bad, but not quite *that* bad.

By the time Dusty emerged, the remainder of the party had come up. Liz, face set and pale, eyes fighting to avoid looking again at the grisly things by the corral, dismounted and walked towards the house.

"Is this Indian work?" she asked, her voice hoarse and strained.

"Yes, ma'am," Dusty replied.

"Was he alone?"

"No."

Listening to Dusty's flat, cold, one-word reply, Liz knew something far worse than the horror at the corral lay in the building. Much as she wanted to turn and run, Liz knew she must see the inside of the cabin. Setting her teeth grimly, she walked by Dusty and before he realised what she meant to do had passed through the door. A low cry left her lips at what she saw. The two children, a boy and a girl, were bad enough, their small bodies battered and mutilated—but the worse horror hung half in, half out of the bed. In life it had been a pretty woman and carrying an unborn child. The face was unmarked. A hideous gash laid the throat open to the bone. Yet there was even more. The woman's belly had been ripped open and the unborn child's body trailed on to the floor by her side.

"This's what they'll turn loose all through Texas," Dusty said quietly.

For a moment Liz stood staring around her. Then she gave a loan moan, turned and collapsed sobbing into Dusty's arms. The cabin seemed to be whirling around, heaving up and down before Liz's eyes and everything went black.

Blue sky greeted her when she recovered. Jill knelt at her side and the rebel girl's face showed concern. To one side Dusty stood talking with Ysabel, and Liz caught the words.

"So it was Kaddo work," he said.

"Sure. Young bucks headed for the council and took a chance to gather some loot," Ysabel agreed. "I didn't figure Comanches'd jump Dutchy, he got on with 'em."

"I should have stopped Liz going in there," Dusty stated.

"Should have," agreed Ysabel. "Only now she knows what Castle's scheme'll mean."

"Yes," Dusty said flatly. "Now she knows. Let's go help the others with the burying."

CHAPTER FOURTEEN

We Owe You That Much, Mr. Marsden

"We're too late, Cap'n," Sam Ysabel told Dusty quietly. "They've beaten us to it. Arrived this morning."

Sitting to one side of the small Texan, Liz listened to the words with a cold chill of apprehension. She had talked little since the finding of the ravaged ranch and her face showed haggard lines not entirely due to fatigue. Watching Dusty, she wondered what he would—or could—do in view of Ysabel's news. They had reached the upper tip of Lake Sheppard and made a hidden camp in the pine woods just below where the Brazos flowed into the lake. On arrival, Dusty sent Ysabel out on a scout of the area, from which the sergeant had just returned and brought the worst possible news.

Liz wondered how Dusty must feel, having ridden so far, planned so well, and to find that he came on the scene just a few hours too late. It must be a bitter blow. Yet she could see no chance of preventing Castle's scheme. Four men and two girls—yes, two, for she intended to give all her help to stopping the uprising—could do nothing against a large camp of Indians who had the backing of an Ager Coffee Mill gun.

"How much do you know?" Dusty asked.

"Caught me a Kaddo buck as he was out hunting," Ysabel answered. "He got around to talking after a spell. The big council's fixed for tonight. Then the Yankees'll be showing off their Devil Gun, which's what they're calling the Ager."

"Is it much of a camp?" asked Billy Jack, mirroring Liz's thoughts.

"I'd put it at around fifty each of Comanches, Kaddos and Kiowas. Few Wacos, smidgin of Attacapas from the coast, and I'd swear to there being some White Mountain Apaches out of New Mexico."

"But how did they all get to hear of the council?" Liz put in.

"Now that's a right smart question, ma'am," Ysabel answered. "I've lived among the Comanches, am a member of the Dog Soldier lodge, but I don't start to pretend I can explain half the things I've seen Injun medicine-men do."

"The meeting's set for tonight, you say, Sam," Dusty said.

"Yep. The chiefs have seen the rifles and only want showing how the Devil Gun works."

"The arms wagon is in the camp?"

"Nope. The Deacon's not that *loco,* Cap'n. He's got it stashed down in the woods on top of the big bend the river makes afore it forks apart. Meeting's right down at the bottom of the bend's loop."

"Many men with the wagon, Sam?" Marsden inquired as he sat at Jill's side.

"The two Yankees, Deacon, his right bower, Cracker and three more. Reckon the Deacon'll take Cracker along when he goes with the Yankees to the Council, seeing's how he don't speak Spanish, and Spanish's the only language that they all understand."

"Leaves three with the wagon then," Billy Jack stated.

"At least we'll stop 'em getting the rifles, Cap'n Dusty."

"And the Injuns'd still ride. More so to get them back. Especially when they see what that Ager'll do," Kiowa informed him.

"If we could only get into that council—" Dusty began.

"We can," Ysabel replied. " 'Least I can. I'm a member of the Dog Soldier lodge and can go to any council called for the tribe."

"Even in your army uniform?" asked Dusty.

"Got my medicine boot for the Sharps, with that it don't matter how I dress. Long Walker's there and he's my friend. If I know him, he don't want this war. He's an old-time Comanche and won't hold with riding alongside Kaddos, much less with Wacos or them coast Attacapas. With him there, I can walk into that council."

"Can you take me in with you?"

For a long moment Ysabel did not reply. Then he nodded his head. "There's one way. If you and I were blood brothers, I could take you along."

"Then you'd best make me your blood brother," Dusty said.

"Have you a plan, sir?" Marsden asked, watching Dusty intently.

"Call it a fool notion, mister," Dusty replied. "I've learned a few things about Indians during this journey. Enough to take a chance on spoiling the Devil Gun's medicine."

Although a painful death awaited him if anything went wrong with Dusty's plan, Billy Jack did not hesitate to ask, "How many of us're going, sir?"

"Only Sam and I," Dusty answered, and stifled the low rumble of objection with a gesture. "Mr. Marsden, you'll take Billy Jack and Kiowa tonight and either bring away that arms wagon, or destroy it. Either way, it must not fall into the Indian's hands."

"And the girls, sir?" Marsden said.

"They will remain here, hidden," Dusty ordered, and

looked at Liz as she made a start at protesting. "No arguments, Miss Chamberlain. Neither of you are trained or suited for the work ahead. I want you to remain here with the pack animals. If we haven't returned at dawn, or if you hear anything to suggest that we won't be coming back, strike out to the south along the river. Ride as you've learned during the journey and when you find white folks start to spread the word of what's happened up here."

"Very good, Captain," Liz replied.

"We'll get through, if we can," Jill promised, trying to hold concern out of her voice as she clung to Marsden's hand.

"Best show us how the land lies around the wagon, Sam," Kiowa suggested.

Squatting on his heels by the fire, Ysabel used his bowie knife's point to clear a patch of earth on which he drew a rough, but fairly accurate map of the arms wagon's location. Using his knowledge of such matters as a guide, he pointed out the easiest route by which to make an advance towards the clearing in which the wagon stood and mentioned the snags one might expect.

"Only things I can see's going to be whether Mr. Marsden and Billy Jack can move quiet enough through the woods in the dark," he concluded. "Them boys guarding the wagon know Injuns and won't be sleeping on the job."

"How about it, Mr. Marsden?" Dusty asked.

"I've hunted deer, sir."

"Deer don't shoot back and take your scalp, mister," Ysabel remarked, but his voice stayed friendly. "You'll have to move *real* quiet through the woods so's to get up close—"

"And then cross about twenty yards of open ground to reach the men," Dusty interrupted, bringing up a point the other overlooked. "They'll have to be taken quietly. I don't want the Indians at the council alerting."

"There's no chance of waiting until the guards sleep,

sir?" asked Marsden. "They might all go to sleep at the same time."

"In *Injun* country?" Ysabel grunted. "I tell you, mister, these fellers know the game. They're still alive and they've been in hostile country most of their growing lives."

Silence dropped on the men for a moment as they began to examine the difficulties of the situation.

"I could get to the edge of the clearing without 'em hearing me," Kiowa stated. "But it's moving in on them that'll make the fuss."

"What we need is a diversion," Marsden put in.

Liz had sat listening to the talk, her brain working furiously in an attempt to help out with the problem. An idea came to her and she looked at Jill for a moment before speaking.

"Perhaps Jill and I could cause the diversion you need," she said and explained her idea.

"It might work," Dusty admitted.

"Won't it be too dangerous for—the girls, sir?" Marsden asked.

"Mister, they're living in danger," Dusty answered. "But it's going to take some slick timing to bring it off. And there's another thing—" At that point his words trailed off and he sat for a few seconds thinking out the idea which came. "There's one way we could play it," he finally remarked.

None of the three men guarding the arms wagon cared for the thought of sitting within two miles of a sizeable Indian camp while in possession of such desirable loot as three hundred Sharps rifles, with ammunition, percussion caps and Maynard tape primers to feed the said weapons. True the various tribes gathered for a peaceful council, but some of the younger bucks might take it into their heads that the top of the big bend of the river did not count as sacred ground and so could be raided with impunity.

So the trio stayed alert, ears strained to catch any deviation from the normal night noises. While the men might lack formal schooling, and their morals left much to be desired, all knew one thing very well; how to stay alive in hostile country. The normal night noises did not disturb them, but a fresh sound came to their ears and brought them to their feet at the small fire on which their coffee pot stood.

"Hosses," announced the lean, bearded man. "Coming this way."

"Only two of 'em," remarked the short, stocky man.

A moment later all three heard the faint click of steel striking rock, although less keen ears would have failed to catch the sound.

"Shod hooves," growled the third of the guards.

No Indian ever rode a shod horse. Even should he take a white man's horse as loot, the Indian ripped off the valuable metal shoes for his own use.

"Get out of sight!" snapped the bearded man. "Hit the wagon, Smokey. You go in the bushes, Will."

Neither questioned the bearded man's right to give orders. Turning, the short man hurried across the clearing and took cover in the bushes on the very edge of the area illuminated by the fire. Moving just as fast, the third man went to the rear of the wagon, swung himself up and disappeared inside. The bearded man threw a glance at the Volcanic rifle which rested against his saddle, then he looked towards the picketed team and saddle horses at one side of the clearing. Finally he sank on his haunches at the fire, drawing his Navy Colt and resting it on his knees.

Nearer came the horses, following the rough trail made by the Deacon on previous trading visits to the bend of the river. If the riders aimed to sneak up on the camp, they showed poor judgment or mighty poor faith in the guards' abilities. Making no attempt to ride quietly, the newcomers came closer, although still out of sight.

"Hello the fire!" called a female voice.

"Who is it?" a second woman's voice went on.

A few seconds later the man found himself gazing at a pair of dishevelled, pretty girls who rode slumped wearily in their saddles. His eyes took in Jill's torn shirt and the fact that she needed one hand to hold the cloth together. From there he gazed with frank interest at Liz, whose blouse had lost a sleeve and hung ripped open down its side, while her skirt was torn from hem almost to hip and showed an expanse of bare white leg as she rode astride.

"Th—Thank God!" Liz gasped. "You're white men. We've been lost for hours until we saw your fire."

Rising, the man eyed the girls suspiciously and made no attempt to holster his gun. "Where'd you come from?" he asked.

"We were travelling to Fort Worth with a party from the Indian Nations," Jill answered. "Only we lost them last night."

"Get down," the man growled.

Instinctively he knew something to be wrong, although he could not quite put his finger on it. Certainly the girls looked weary, untidy and scared enough to have been lost for some time. Maybe—

At that point he lost his interest in the matter. Liz started to swing her leg over the saddle and dismount, but the torn hem of her skirt caught on the horn and hung there. A squeal of embarrassment left her lips as she lowered her foot to the ground and found her leg exposed to view.

When dressing for her part in Dusty's plan, Liz donned the clothing damaged in her first fight with Jill and augmented it with a pair of very daring drawers of a kind actresses, but few of Liz's class, wore. She thought the effect might be increased by the extra exposure the drawers offered as opposed to the more ladylike long-legged variety a proper young lady wore. From the way the bearded man's eyes bulged, she knew she'd made a wise decision.

"I—I'm caught up," she told the man pathetically.

Watching Liz, Jill could barely hold down a chuckle. Give her her due, the Yankee girl could sure act. She looked as helpless as the heroine of one of the melodramatic plays put on by travelling theatrical troupes; although they never showed their legs in so daring a manner during mixed or family shows. Certainly the bearded man had no suspicions as he started forward to help free Liz's skirt.

Nor, it appeared, had the other two guards. In an age when a woman's exposed calf drew gasps of indignation, or interested stares, depending on the sex of the observer, men like that trio would not hesitate to take a closer look at as much exposed female limb as Liz offered to view.

Dropping from the wagon, Smokey walked towards the girls. He failed to see why Rogers should have all the fun. So did Will, for he emerged from the bushes and started to hurry across the clearing. In his haste, Will failed to notice a dark shape rise behind him and follow on his trail with the silent, deadly purpose of a cougar stalking a white-tailed deer. In one respect Will might have counted himself fortunate. While awaiting the girls' arrival, Kiowa watched Will's arrival in the bushes. Knife in hand, the Indian-dark sergeant stalked Will and had been on the point of silencing the other when Will left cover to lend a hand with Liz's predicament. Silently, Kiowa glided out of the woods after Will and only the other's preoccupation with viewing Liz's legs prevented his normally keen senses from detecting his danger.

Although as absorbed in the view as his two friends were, Rogers could not help but feel that he missed an important detail. Not until he had almost reached Liz did he realise what was wrong. While the girls showed signs of hard traveling, their horses appeared to be fresh.

"What the—" he began.

At which point Billy Jack and Marsden burst into sight from either side of the trail down which the girls appeared. Guns in hand, they sprang forward, covering the startled guards.

"Freeze, boys!" Billy Jack requested.

Rogers let out a low snarl and his hand stabbed down at

his gun. Jumping her buckskin forward, Jill swung up the hand she kept hidden from the guards. In it she held her Tranter and she put the gun to good use. Up rose her hand and, powered by a strong arm, slammed the barrel of the gun downwards on to Rogers' head. Giving a low grunt, the man buckled at the knees and went down.

Exposed to the guns of the newcomers far more than Rogers had been, Smokey raised his hands in surrender. While a shot might alert the boss' party at the big council, Smokey knew its bullet would end his life; and he did not feel in the mood for noble self-sacrifice right then.

Across the clearing, Will reached hip-wards. He figured himself to be far enough from the soldiers to take a chance and also that they could not see his movement. Even as his fingers closed around the butt of his gun, his instincts told him that he was not alone. The feeling received confirmation when something sharp pricked his spine just at the point where the kidneys could best be reached by an exploratory knife.

"Let's keep it quiet, *hombre*," growled an Indian-savage voice in Will's ear. "Just walk forward slow and easy."

A hand removed Will's gun, tossing it aside, and he walked forward slowly.

"It worked," Liz announced proudly, freeing her dress and letting it drop into something like a respectable position.

"Never thought it wouldn't," Billy Jack replied as he advanced to disarm the other guards.

Nor had he, for he possessed great faith in the planning ability of the small man who led him. Dusty's idea worked smoothly. To give them a chance to approach the camp undetected, Dusty told Marsden and Billy Jack to ride behind the girls and drop off the horses just before reaching the clearing. In that way they avoided a long, difficult stalk through the woods with the danger of making some noise to warn the guards. How well the plan worked showed as the Deacon's men lost their weapons without a shot being fired or an unnecessary noise made.

"Tie them securely, Sergeant-major," Marsden ordered, and wondered if the man would obey him.

"Yo!" Billy Jack replied.

While Marsden might be a Yankee, Billy Jack had received Dusty's orders to let Marsden command the party and the lean non-com needed no more than that. Swiftly but thoroughly Billy Jack and Kiowa roped their prisoners' hands and feet. With that done, Kiowa grinned at Liz.

"How's about showing us how you got these jaspers watching you, when we get back to the regiment, ma'am?" he asked.

"I thought you saw just now," she answered, trying to think if she had ever seen the impassive man smile before.

"I did, only a feller can allus learn if he sees a thing done enough."

"Sure can," Billy Jack chuckled. "Let's hitch up the wagon and pull out."

"Say," Kiowa drawled as they led the team horses into position. "These rifles will sure come in handy for our infantry."

"They sure will," Billy Jack agreed.

Suddenly Marsden realised what the words meant. If the Texans took the arms wagon back to Arkansas, the rifles would be used against the Union Army, probably to kill members of his regiment. A grim, tight expression came to his face.

"We'll throw the rifles and ammunition over that cliff into the lake," he said. "There's nearly thirty foot of water under it, Sergeant Ysabel said as we passed it. The Indians will never recover them from there."

An angry objection rose to both Texans' lips, but died unsaid. For the first time in days they remembered that Marsden served the Union. Yet they also knew what his presence meant to the people of Texas. Billy Jack and

Kiowa exchanged glances, then the sergeant-major nodded.

"We owe you that much, Mr. Marsden," he said.

"How about the prisoners?" Marsden asked, to conceal his gratitude and relief.

"We'll turn them loose. With the guns gone, they'll know what to expect if the Indians lay hands on them," Kiowa replied. "Wonder how Cap'n Dusty's doing?"

CHAPTER FIFTEEN

Let Them Kill Me With Their Devil Gun

In many ways the Ager Coffee Mill Gun was a fine weapon, far superior to the Barnes or Ripley guns which preceded it and better, more reliable than the Billinghurst Requa or Vandenburg Volley gun. The model in Castle and Silverman's possession stood on a light artillery mount, but lacked the protective shield fitted to some models as defence for the gunners against return fire by the enemy. Single barrelled, .58 in calibre, it derived its name from the resemblance its operating parts bore to the coffee-grinding mills of the day.

Standing to the left of the gun, Lieutenant Silverman fed another handful of loaded chargers into the hopper-shaped magazine on top of the gun. The sallow-faced, large-nosed stocky lieutenant made sure each charger went in correctly, for both he and his partner in the scheme knew they must not let the Indians see the gun jam.

Captain Castle, at the gun's right side, twirled its cranking handle at less than the fastest possible speed. Far from a source of supply, he wanted to conserve powder, shot and chargers as much as possible. While the guns fired slowly, it still exceeded anything the Indians had ever seen. Mutters of awe rose all around the half-circle of watching chiefs and braves as the gun continued to crash, spewing its used chargers around the tall, slim, lean-faced captain's feet.

At last Castle stopped turning the handle, although several rounds still remained in the hopper. By the time he had turned towards the Indians, he found their usual impassive masks looking at him and he read nothing on their faces. Running a tongue tip over his lips in a nervous manner, Castle turned his gaze to the two civilians who stood on his right. Tall, gaunt, clad in the garb of a circuit-riding preacher, the Deacon's somber features showed as little expression as the Indians'. He stood with legs braved apart, an eight gauge, twin barrelled shotgun held down before him in both hands. Next to the Deacon lounged a lean, long-haired, dirty, mean-faced man in smoke-blackened buckskins, but the gunbelt around his waist and the holstered Army Colt were clean and cared-for.

An elderly, stocky, powerfully built Comanche chief growled out a question and Cracker turned to Castle.

"Long Walker says the Devil Gun eats much powder and shot. Can you get more?"

Bending down, Castle lifted one of the used chargers and held it for the chief—one of the most powerful and influential present—to see. The charger proved to be a steel tube with a place in its bottom to accommodate a percussion cap. Taking the powder flask and moulded lead bullet from Silverman's reluctant hand—the lieutenant hoped to heighten his prestige by demonstrating how to load the charger, but Castle did not intend to allow anyone to share his glory. The captain showed the Indian how easily the Devil Gun's appetite could be appeased.

"Tell the chief that we will have powder, lead and fresh charges brought as we need them," Castle ordered Cracker. "We have enough for an attack upon both Fort Worth and

Dallas, after we have proved our claims for the gun on some smaller-objective."

While Cracker interpreted, Castle stood thinking of his great scheme. Once the Indians rose, there would be no stopping them and they would wipe out the hated rebels. That ought to bring the Texans fighting in the Confederate Army home with a rush, but they would not arrive in one party and the Indians ought to be able to swamp, then exterminate each body of men as it returned. That loss of man-power would so weaken the South that it must surrender. Castle wished there was some way the Indians could be turned loose through all the Southern States so as to leave none of the rebels alive.

At that point of his day-dream, Castle became aware of a stir among the assembled Indians and a startled gasp from Silverman. Bringing his eyes in the direction everybody stared, the Union captain let his mouth drop open at what he saw.

Two men walked from the darkness which surrounded the area lit by large fires. Not just two men, but a pair of Confederate soldiers, a captain and a sergeant, in uniform. Unlike the two Union officers, who showed a voluntary untidiness beyond that of hard travel, Dusty Fog looked smart; for Jill and Liz had worked hard all day to clean up the signs of the journey from his clothes. To show their 'good faith' the two Yankees attended the meeting without weapons. From what Ysabel told him. Dusty retained his gunbelt as a sign that he respected the others present and expected them to be able to trust him among them while armed.

Up lunged a Kaddo brave, lifting the Hawkens rifle from his knees. Before he could make a move, one of his companions caught his arm and pointed to the fringed, decorated buckskin boot which covered Ysabel's rifle.

"This one is called Ysabel!" boomed Long Walker in a warning voice. "He is a member of the Dog Soldier lodge as his medicine pouch shows."

Which meant that the big white man had a right to attend the council and anyone who objected chanced the wrath of the most feared of all the Comanche war lodges.

"And the other?" asked Plenty Kills, main chief of the Kiowa.

"This one is a great war chief of his people," Ysabel answered in Spanish. "He is my blood brother, we cut wrists and mixed blood."

And that gave Dusty the right to be present.

"What do you want here?" Lone Hunter of the Kaddo asked.

For the first time in his life the Deacon panicked. Knowing his fate at the hands of his fellow Texans should his betrayal become public news, he prepared to take the easy way out, relying on the Devil Gun's medicine to quieten any Indian-raised objections to his breach of hospitality.

"They're spies!" he screeched and started to lift his shotgun. "Get 'em!"

Instantly Cracker sent his right hand stabbing towards the butt of his gun. He knew Sam Ysabel could never removed the long medicine boot from the Sharps in time to take a hand, which left only that rebel captain to be handled.

An instant behind Cracker's move, Dusty sent his hands crossing to the white handles of the matched Army Colts in a flicker of movement almost faster than the eye could follow. Three-quarters of a second later the two Colts crashed in Dusty's grip, their shots sounding so close together that no man, not even the most quick-eared Indian present, could tell the sound apart. Caught between the eyes with a .44 bullet, the Deacon pitched over backwards, his shotgun still not raised high enough to fire. Colt still in leather, Cracker rocked, spun around and fell even as his boss went down.

A low mutter arose from the watching Indians, but interest and not anger prompted it. Every man present was a brave-heart warrior with a name for being a bone-tough fighter from soda to hock. The quickest and most effective way to gain their attention was to display superlative skill in the handling of any kind of weapon. Every man present realised they watched a master hand demonstrate his talent in the business of killing enemies.

"This one is called Magic Hands," Ysabel boomed out as Dusty holstered the guns. "He comes to the council to listen and speak."

Long Walker looked around the party of leading chiefs with whom he sat. First Plenty Kills, an old friend of the Comanche chief, nodded in agreement. Not to be out-done in courtesy and adherence to tradition, the other chiefs gave their complete assent to Dusty's continued presence.

Remembering what Ysabel told him about Indian etiquette, Dusty turned to Castle and saluted.

"Carry on speaking, sir," he said.

Confusion and distrust showed on Castle's face as he received Dusty's permission and watched the small Texan walk over to sit among the chiefs. Then he saw a way out of the predicament.

"I can't speak Spanish."

"Sergeant Ysabel will interpret for you," Dusty countered.

"I said all I meant to before you came," Castle snarled.

"And I heard you," Dusty replied. "With your permission, sir, I'll speak to the council now you're through."

Once more a low rumble went around the assembled Indians. Tradition meant much to them and they respected a man who showed courtesy to an enemy. All would listen to Dusty the more willingly now he had shown his knowledge of their ways.

Stepping forward, Dusty looked around at the sea of impassive brown faces. After a moment's thought to prepare himself for speaking in Spanish, he began to address the council.

"The blue-coat chief says you should attack the settlements. You have tried before and many brave-hearts now roam the land of the spirits. He says many of our men are away, fighting with his people. That is true, but they can return soon and will come bringing many wheel guns—"

"You have the Devil Gun!" Castle yelled, for Ysabel had been translating Dusty's words for the Yankee's benefit. In doing so Castle committed a breach of council etiquette, he should have waited for Dusty to finish before speaking.

"The Devil Gun is only one. We have many wheel guns," Dusty went on.

Again Castle burst in. "The Devil Gun is here. The greycoats' wheel guns are far away."

While Ysabel turned Castle's words into Spanish, Dusty thought up an answer.

"This chief thinks much of the Devil Gun's medicine. But has he showed you proof that its medicine is good?"

"I fired the gun." Castle answered edging nearer to the trap Dusty set for him. "All men here saw its power."

Like a flash Dusty cut back with. "All men heard noises. But children in their games make noises and do no harm."

"You've seen the gun work!" Castle yelled.

"But you have not seen it kill!" Dusty pointed out and he walked slowly around to halt some twenty feet before the muzzle of the gun. "Let them kill me with their Devil Gun—if its medicine is strong enough to do so."

Although Castle knew no Spanish, he understood Dusty's gesture without needing Ysabel's explanation. A quick glance around the council showed him a tense expectancy and he knew that he must accept the Texan's challenge. On the face of it everything was in Castle's favour. He stood at the side of the gun still, its firing handle close to his hand. All he need do was reach forward, grip and move that handle to send a bullet into Dusty's stomach. Such a simple thing to do.

And then Castle remembered how the Deacon and Cracker came to die!

They too thought they had an easy task on their hands. Almost as if it happened again, Castle saw the way the small Texan's hands moved to draw, shoot and kill the two renegades.

When Castle conceived his scheme, he saw himself following in the wake of the attacking Indians, using the Ager from a safe distance and taking no chances. Running risks with his valuable life did not enter his calculations. He planned to stay alive to reap the acclaim and benefits the successful end of the plan would bring. Only he would not do so if he tried to reach the gun's firing handle.

"It's your turn to handle the gun, Herbie," he told Silverman.

Shock, fear and suspicion mingled on Silverman's face at the words. Like most of his kind, Silverman had a mean-minded, mistrusting nature, and also a very broad steak of caution. Killing people without a chance did not worry him, but trying to kill a man who could move as quickly as Dusty did, brought a muck-sweat of apprehension to the Union lieutenant.

"It was your idea," he hissed back to Castle. "You do it."

A rustle of movement ran through the council as the two Yankees hesitated to display the Devil Gun's medicine. Through it all Dusty stood still, hands at his sides, face showing complete assurance that should Castle make a move, Dusty knew he could beat it. After almost two minutes Dusty took his plan a step further. Slowly he reached down and unfastened the holsters' pigging thongs from around his legs.

"Perhaps the Devil Gun's medicine does not work against armed men," he said.

Shocked, disbelief etched itself upon Ysabel's usually impassive face as he saw, though could hardly believe, what Dusty aimed to do. Ysabel's agitation showed even more as he gave a low-growled warning.

"You'll have to go through with it if you once start, Cap'n."

"I aim to, Sam," Dusty replied and unbuckled his belt. "I aim to."

With that, Dusty tossed his guns to one side and stood empty handed before the yawning muzzle of the Devil Gun. However, he gave the impression of being ready to dive after and grab his guns should Castle make a move.

Sucking in his breath, Castle took a chance. He lunged forward, reaching for the firing handle with his right hand, the left swinging the gun on its lateral traverse. Crouching slightly, Castle aimed the Ager's barrel downwards so that it moved in line towards where Dusty's gunbelt lay. Around turned the handle, flame spurting out—to strike nothing but earth.

Dusty had not dived for his guns—he never meant to do so. At Castle's first movement, Dusty went forward in a rolling dive, straight towards the left side of the Ager. While Castle swung the gun towards the right, Dusty passed from its range of fire and to comparative safety.

Letting out a yell in which fear and fury mingled, Silverman sprang from his place at the loading hopper to land kneeling at Dusty's right and grab down at the Texan's throat with both hands. Castle, filled with concern for his safety, and mortification, plunged around the Ager and prepared to launch a vicious kick at Dusty from the other side.

Realising that he must deal with Silverman first, Dusty went into action long before Castle made his move. Even as Silverman's hands reached his throat, Dusty's left leg rose and its knee smashed into the Yankee's ribs. A grunt of pain burst from Silverman and his hold relaxed slightly. Up shot Dusty's right arm, passing between Silverman's as it aimed towards the other's face. Instead of clenching his fist, Dusty kept the fingers extended and held together, thumb bent across his palm in the *nukite* piercing hand of karate. The tips of his fingers stabbed hard under Silverman's nose, catching the philtrum collection of nerve centres. Although unable to put all his power behind the blow, Dusty still brought about a rapid release of his throat and left himself free to handle Castle's impending assault.

Rolling over on to his left side, Dusty struck around with his left arm. He used the *uraken* back-fist blow to hit and deflect Castle's kicking leg. On the heels of the *uraken*, Dusty's right hand stabbed forward to catch Castle's raised ankle and heaved to unbalance the Yankee. Drawing up his left leg under him, Dusty lashed out a snap kick with his right that just missed Castle's groin and sent him reeling away.

Dusty began to rise, conscious of the admiring mutters from the watching Indians. Before he made his feet properly, Dusty saw Silverman come in with a swinging fist. Unable to avoid the blow, Dusty took it and went crashing into the Ager's wheel. Springing forward in a concerted rush, Castle and Silverman each grabbed hold of Dusty's jacket front with one hand while smashing the other into his face or body. Unable to retreat, Dusty threw up his left hand in a sweeping-block move, its edge chopping into Castle's arm and preventing the fist reaching his face. At the same moment Dusty drove back his right arm, to use a pressing-block that held Silverman's attempt to hit his stomach. Such was the strength of Dusty's small frame that he held both bigger men's blows, actually pinning Silverman's hand against the lieutenant's body with is blocking blow. Releasing hold of Dusty's jacket, Castle sprang back to try another line of attack.

"Hold him, Herbie!" he yelled.

If it came to a point, Dusty held Silverman; for his pressing-block kept the other's disengaged arm immobile. Castle came in, throwing a savage right at Dusty's head. Pivoting to face the danger, Dusty retained his pressing-block on Silverman and knocked aside Castle's blow with his left arm, following it with a smashing jolt of his right elbow into the Yankee captain's chest. Croaking in pain, Castle staggered backwards and gave Dusty a chance to deal with Silverman. Like a flash Dusty delivered a kick to the rear, stamping his boot heel against Silverman's shin. So quickly had everything happened that Silverman's brain could not cope with the situation and issue orders. The impact of Dusty's boot against Silverman's leg prevented the need for thought. With a yelp, the stocky lieutenant released his hold and hopped away on one leg.

Leaping forward, Castle swung a roundhouse blow towards Dusty's head. Dusty saw the danger, ducked under the punch, sank a right into Castle's belly and jack-knifed him over. Driving up his knee, Dusty caught Castle's down-dropping face and jerked him erect. Whipping across his left Dusty smashed home a punch which spun the Yankee around and sent him sprawling to the ground in front of the Ager gun. Before Dusty could make a move to handle any further developments, Silverman leapt in from behind him and curled arms around the small Texan in a full nelson hold. Fear and desperation lent strength to Silverman's arms and Dusty grunted as the hold sent pain knifing into him.

"Carnie!" Silverman screeched. "Do something!"

The words bit through Castle's spinning senses and as his eyes regained focus they rested on a possible salvation. Not far ahead of him lay the Texan's gunbelt, its white-handled Colt burden showing like providence to Castle's eyes. Ignoring his companion's cry, he flung himself forward, hands reaching towards the butt of the nearest gun.

Once again Dusty had thought faster than his enemy. Recognising the danger, he prepared to handle it. First he must free himself, and he knew he could not do it quickly enough by matching arm strength with Silverman. So he did not try. Drawing forward his body, Dusty propelled it back, driving his buttocks into Silverman's lower belly with enough force to cause an immediate release. Moaning, Silverman reeled backwards and Dusty ignored him for the moment.

Bounding forward, Dusty reached the Ager. He took quick sight and whirled the firing handle even as Castle's hands hovered over The butt of the nearer Colt. Loud in the night rose the chatter of the Devil Gun's repeated explosions; flame belched from its barrel. A line of dust-spurts rose, creeping closer to Castle's body. He turned a horrified face towards the gun, mouth dropping open and trying to speak. The bullets crawled closer and closer, throwing up dirt as they ploughed into the ground. Then no more dirt rose. Castle jerked as the first bullet struck his body. Five more .58 balls tore into him before Dusty could halt the Devil Gun's fire. Torn almost in half by the lead, Castle's lifeless body pitched over and lay still.

Dusty left the gun, whirling to meet any attack Silverman launched. Although a good three inches taller and much heavier than Dusty, Silverman lacked the guts to continue the fight. Turning, he started to run—and made a fatal mistake. While the Indian admired and respected a brave man, he had nothing but contempt for a coward. Giving a low, disgusted grunt, one of the watching braves bounded up as Silverman approached. Out thrust a buffalo lance, its point ripping into Silverman's body. The stocky lieutenant let out a croaking scream and fell, writhing out the remainder of his life and shedding his blood upon the Texas plains he had hoped to redden with the gore of the Southerners he hated.

Leaning on the side of the Ager gun, Dusty fought to regain his breath. He heard the rumbling approval of the watching Indians and saw Sam Ysabel springing towards him. Regaining his breath, Dusty waved Ysabel aside and faced the assembled tribal chiefs.

"The Devil Gun's medicine is bad," he stated. "It did not protect the blue-coats."

"But it killed well," Plenty Kills remarked, pointing to Castle's body.

"It killed the man who would have used it, not me," Dusty pointed out. "And should you take it to war, the same would happen to you. The blue-coat lied when he said the Devil Gun would bring you victory. We have wheel guns which could shoot from far away and smash it. And if you ride to war, which tribe takes the Devil Gun?"

There Dusty posed a problem to the Indians. No one tribe would willingly allow any other to be in possession of such a deadly weapon. Talk welled up. Hostile glares passed among the various tribal enemies. Not for five minutes could Ysabel make himself heard to put forward his flash of inspiration. At last silence fell and all eyes went to the big, burly sergeant with the war lodge sheath on his rifle.

"Who owns the Devil Gun now the blue-coats are dead?" he asked, but gave his audience no time to answer. "Among all true man the brave who counts the coup takes the loot and keeps it. Of course among the poor-spirited people like the Tejas,* such is not done."

Put that way, no Texas Indian with pride in the honour of his tribe could object to Dusty retaining ownership of the Ager; not when watched by critical members of the other tribes. If only one tribe had been present, its members might have changed the wrath of the Great Spirit at failing to give a warrior his due, and killed Dusty to gain possession of the Devil Gun. As Ysabel well knew, no race-proud Indian would lower his tribal honour by doing so before witnesses from another nation.

"What do you do with the Devil Gun, Magic Hands?" asked Long Walker in good English.

"It's medicine is bad," Dusty replied. "No true man wants such a thing to fight for him."

"You fixing to take it with us, Cap'n?" Ysabel inquired, bringing Dusty his gunbelt.

*Tejas: Texas tribe noted for friendship with the white men.

Much as the South could use such a weapon, Dusty knew what he must do. To take the Ager would be asking for trouble. He knew that once clear of the council area one of the tribes, or a bunch of name-making young braves from it, might decide to take the gun for the use of their people. If Dusty attempted to return to Arkansas with the Ager, he could expect trouble all the way.

"See if there is any powder in the caisson, Sergeant," he said.

Without another word, Ysabel turned and went to where the Ager gun's caisson stood. The caisson, a two-wheeled ammunition carrier fitted with the necessary parts so a team of horses could be harnessed to it, proved to hold two twenty-five pound kegs of du Pont black powder, spare chargers and molded bullets. Taking out the kegs, one of which had been opened, Ysabel carried them to Dusty. Taking the unopened keg, Dusty placed it under the wheels of the gun. Next he used some of the contents of the open keg and lay a trail of powder from the full keg to some twenty feet away. Returning to the Ager, Dusty set the used keg at the end of the trail, making sure a continuous line of powder ran to it. He walked back to the end of the powder trail, accepted the match offered by Ysabel and rasped it alight on the seat of his pants. Nobody spoke, not one of the Indians moved, as they watched Dusty place the flame on the end of the powder trail. Flame spurted up, crawling along the ground until it came to the two kegs. Loud in the night came the roar as some thirty pounds of black powder exploded. For a moment the watching Indians were blinded by the glare. When their eyes cleared again, they found the Devil Gun to be wrecked beyond any hope of repair.

"Reckon that's that," breathed Ysabel, relief plain in his voice.

"Like you say, Sergeant," Dusty answered. "Now all we have to do is get out of here."

"That'll cause no fuss," grinned Ysabel. "Just look at all them chiefs rushing up all excited to meet you."

Watching the slow, dignified manner in which the chiefs rose and walked towards him, Dusty found it hard to imagine anything less rushing or excited in appearance.

"That's all rushing and excited?" he asked.

"Sure is," agreed Ysabel. "For Injuns that is. Usually they'd sit back and let you make first move."

"You fight well, Magic Hands," said Long Walker, halting before Dusty and offering his hand to be shaken white man's fashion. "Aiee! You might be a Comanche."

"Never have I seen such a way of fighting," enthused Plenty Kills, not to be out-done in the matter of showing respect to a great warrior.

"It was a remembered fight," Lone Hunter went on, "and would have been the greater if the blue-coats fought better."

A rumble of agreement rose from the other chiefs, but all made it clear that they did not blame Dusty for any discrepancies the fight showed. Then came promises that no concerted, inter-tribal action would be made against the whites in Texas.

"But the young men will still raid," warned Long Walker in the apologetic tone of one who explains an obvious point to a social equal. "That is always the way. How else can the young man make his name as a warrior, or win trophies to buy many squaws? It is a pity you can have but one woman, Magic Hands. You would have many white maidens wanting you to buy them."

"It is no pity," stated Plenty Kills. "If Magic Hands had plenty squaws, they would give him many sons like himself and the white-eyes could then drive us from our lands with ease."

The compliments continued, each chief trying to excel the others in their praise for a brave fighting man who might one day be a potential enemy. Standing before the chiefs, Dusty tried to stay impassive and hide his pleasure at the praise. He felt grateful that none of his kin or brother officers heard some of the things said in his praise.

Finally each chief gave his word that none of his people would impede Dusty's party during their return to Arkansas.

"Ask them for a relay of horses, Cap'n," Ysabel suggested. "Then I can go on ahead of you to tell General Hardin how things've turned out."

While Dusty had thought of the possibility of sending a man ahead with his report, he hesitated to ask Ysabel to take the task. It meant an even more hard and gruelling ride than the trip out and Dusty wanted a volunteer to make the journey. Having his volunteer, he made the request. Eagerly the chiefs offered the pick of their horse herds and Ysabel selected three fine, powerful horses which, along with his roan, ought to be able to cover fifty miles a day given anything like reasonable conditions.

The next morning Dusty and his small band turned east, following the wake of the faster-travelling Ysabel and leaving the Indian council to disband. Although Dusty did not hear of it until many years later, a picked escort of Comanche Dog Soldiers trailed his party from a distance ready to lend a hand should any other tribe break its word.

With each day of the journey to the east, the Texans grew more relaxed and cheerful at the thought of returning to their friends. Liz gradually threw off the shock of seeing the Indian-massacred family and tried to raise Marsden's spirits, without much success. Each day Marsden grew more quiet and disturbed, for the return to Arkansas meant that he must face his own kind and stand his trial as a traitor. In love with Jill, wanting to make her his wife and devote his life to making her happy, he knew that he stood but little chance of being allowed to do so.

CHAPTER SIXTEEN

Marsden's Fate

Lieutenant Jackson Hardin Marsden never stood trial for either desertion or treason. On his return to Arkansas, he was taken under a flag of truce to the Ouachita River and passed into the care of a colonel from the U.S. Adjutant General's Department. After a thorough interrogation of Marsden, reading a bulky letter sent by General Hardin, and interviews with Liz Chamberlain and Jill Dodd, the colonel took Marsden to Little Rock, from where the lieutenant found himself detailed to join a west-bound supply train and transferred to a cavalry regiment serving in the Montana Territory. With Marsden when he went, travelled Mrs. Marsden; until recently Jill Dodd, Confederate sympathiser, ex-bushwhacker band member and hater of everything to do with the Union. Far from the civil conflict, she managed to make her husband happy; and even forgot her old hatreds.

What brought about the Union's remarkable leniency towards Marsden?

A number of things.

First, Ole Devil Hardin's report of the affair reached

General Handiman at the Adjutant General's Department and from him went to Sherman, Grant and finally into President Lincoln's hands. The latter, great man that he was, saw the full implications and cost in innocent lives of Castle's scheme. He also visualised the effect word that such a scheme had been tried might have upon world opinion. At that time the United States strove to improve its public image—although the term had not then come into use—in the eyes of the European countries. The United States' prestige had dwindled in Europe after a U.S. Navy ship stopped a British merchantman on the high seas and forcibly removed several accredited Confederate ambassadors and other officials. Feelings ran high in Britain at the breach of diplomatic immunity and insult to her flag, and the United Nations feared that what was then the greatest power in the world might swing its weight fully behind the Confederacy. Even now the situation hung in a delicate balance. Should word of the attempted arming of Indians and endangering of innocent civilians leak out, the Confederate propagandists in Europe would have fuel to burn against the Union. Ole Devil hinted in his letter to Handiman that any attempt to court martial Marsden would see the full facts placed in the hands of various European military observers who visited the combat zones.

After some deliberation, a decision came down that Marsden had acted for the best. Colonel Stedloe of the Zouaves received a letter which left him in no doubt of how the top brass regarded his permitting the scheme. In the same package came orders transferring Marsden to the Eighth Cavalry who kept the peace with—or against—the Indians in Montana Territory. The order was dated the day before Marsden deserted, turned traitor—and helped save thousands of men, women, and children from death at the hands of Indians inspired by the evil medicine of the Devil Gun.